Ben Bones and the Conventional Murders

Michael F. Havelin

A Ben Bones Genealogical Adventure

Copyright 2015 by Michael F. Havelin
All rights reserved.

Written, designed and published by
Michael F. Havelin
Asheville, NC 28816

ISBN-13: 978-0-9853553-5-7

ISBN-10: 0985355352

Paperback

Author's Disclaimer

This book is a work of fiction. Because of the limited time frame within which the story happens, certain liberties had to be taken. These include the speed with which Ben Bones conducts his research, and may also include a variety of sources not yet available to real life genealogists.
Please enjoy the story for what it is:
pure entertainment with a genealogical twist.

Look for other Ben Bones genealogical adventures
at your favorite ebook stores.

Read the entire series.
Info on Ben Bones mysteries can be found at:
http://www.benbones.com

Dedication

To Asheville, Cesspool of Sin.

Acknowledgements

Ruth Dilling of the Old Buncombe County Genealogical Society, for her help with bastardy bond research, her helpful suggestions, and general support.

Scott Dillin, Esq., an Asheville attorney in criminal defense practice and a long-time friend, for his information on police procedure and legal process in the local courts.

Zoe Rhine, Reference Librarian in the North Carolina Room in Pack Library, Asheville, NC, for guidance in finding the numerous details that add to the veracity of this tale.

Asheville Police Officer Adam-24, for his help with Asheville 10-codes and radio protocols.

Sam Spade. You know who I mean, right?

The WNCMysterians, my mystery writers' critique group in Asheville, North Carolina, for their insightful assistance with plot issues, story flow, and plain old English. Check them out at http://www.wncmysterians.org.

Ben Bones himself, the fellow who provides my inspiration. Check him out at http://www.benbones.com.

Jennie Tursh, my biological grandmother who I never knew. The search for her started me out on the genealogical road.

Table of Contents

Day 1 – Thursday

Chapter 1 – Welcome, Conventioneers

I didn't see the guy before he struck. Since there were two of us and only one of him, his tactic was to take one of us out and then confront the other. Nadia was the first. He poked her in the back with a 3-foot length of metal pipe and then hit her on the head with several fast-paced blows. Nadia collapsed to the pavement without a whimper. Then the guy turned on me and we faced off.

"Just empty your pockets, man. Now! Drop it all on the sidewalk!" He waggled the pipe in front of my face. I was vibrating all over from the adrenalin rush, but his hands were shaking even more than mine. His basketball sneakers with the Day-Glo emerald green laces shuffled on the pavement. His dreadlock mane danced in the light of the full moon that cut down through Chicken Alley. I looked at him with what could only have been a startled expression. He whipped the pipe to the side of my head. Wham! I fell to my knees.

"Hurry up! Your pockets!" He rumbled in a hot whisper.

I fumbled for my loose change, but I couldn't find my pocket.

"Your wallet, man! Your wallet!" He waved the pipe at my face and then tapped the ground in front of me several times. I was having a hard time focusing. The three muggers danced in front of me . . . wait a minute . . . there was only one of him a second ago. Nah. Couldn't be. I simply wasn't that drunk. They swung their lengths of pipe at me together, like a choreographed ballet move. And they all connected.

"Come on! I'm short on time, man!" He was getting more jittery, his head swiveling this way and that looking for witnesses. But we were alone in Chicken Alley, and it was after business hours. He was safe enough. Nadia and I sure weren't.

I guess the guy got fed up then. He looked around again, quickly but furtively, poked me in the face with the end of the pipe, and ran off down the unlit mews into the night, his dark dreadlocks bouncing, his baggy cargo pants flapping in the cool night air.

I shook my head to clear it, but I was seeing in multiples. Nadia lay to my left, her skimpy sequined skirt scrunched high up, exposing her shapely athletic legs. I fell toward her, grabbed her leg and shook it. She didn't respond. I shook her again, harder. She still didn't respond, and my head suddenly cleared from the additional burst of adrenalin her lack of response had given me. Adrenalin will trump alcohol every time.

Nadia wasn't moving. She wasn't breathing. I felt her neck for a pulse. There was none.

Hell of a way to kick off a conference, I thought as I collapsed in a heap next to her. Asheville might be a nice place to live, but I didn't like getting mugged in these ancient mountains any better than I would have anywhere else.

***

"What about this one?"

I blinked, and blinked again, but I wasn't back to full clarity yet. A Valkyrie in a grey EMS jacket was shaking me awake by the shoulder. The brick walls of the alley around us pulsed in blue and red flashes, the weird farm scene mural full of chickens on the alley wall looking even more surreal. I tried to sit up.

"Wait a second, bud. Looks like you had a couple of whacks on the head." She held her hand up in front of my face. "How many fingers am I holding up?"

"It's only one hand, but you've got too many fingers." I winced. "I've got a headache."

She rested her big hand crablike but gently on my chest. "Then you stay right where you are for a few minutes, honey, while I check you out." She pulled a stethoscope out of somewhere and listened to my lungs and carotids. She poked me here and there. It tickled. "Any pains anywhere else? Your chest? Your arms? Legs?"

"No. Just a headache."

Both of her gave me a quizzical look. And then, like you'd say to a two-year old, "Wiggle your feet for me."

I waggled my feet back and forth. They worked.

"On a scale of zero to ten," her litany began, "with zero being no pain and ten being your worst pain ever, where are you, darlin'?"

"Maybe four? Five? Five and a half. Six? Six point five." It was a hard question to answer. "Yeah, around there somewhere."

"We're going to transport you to the hospital so a doctor can find out how bad it is. Y'know, take a scan of your head to see if it's broken."

I had a terrible thought. "My insurance. In my wallet. I'm not sure…"

"Don't worry about a thing, sweetheart. You're in good hands."

I began to recollect. "What about Nadia? How's Nadia?"

A sigh. "She's got her own problems," the EMT said soberly. "Don't worry about her. We're taking care of her, too."

I looked around. To my left, a tall, lean EMT in grey was covering a body with a sheet.

"Is that her? What happened? Did that guy…?"

"A guy?" a rasping male voice asked. "What guy? Was anyone with him? Can you describe him, sir?"

A big black man in a dark suit had materialized to loom behind the EMT who crouched over me. His intensity was disturbing.

"What did he look like? Was he black or white? What was he wearing?"

I tried to think. "Y'know, I didn't notice if he was black or white. Might've been somewhere in between. All I saw was those dreadlocks and that pipe he was waving at me. That's what he hit me with, right? A piece of pipe?"

"And your girlfriend too, probably."

"She's not my girlfriend," I said.

"Then who was she? You pick her up in a bar?"

"Well, sort of. You see, we're . . ."

"What bar was that, sir?"

"You think you want to give me a chance to answer one question at a time?" This guy was bugging me.

"Look'a here, sir," he said. "This ain't the murder capital of the U.S. of A., but we got a fresh one here and I already been up 36 hours. If you have a straight answer to give, I'll take it."

"Come on, Wilbur," the Valkyrie broke in. "This guy's got a knot on his head big as a soccer ball. He probably can't see straight, let alone think straight,"

Wilbur shrugged. "I'm tired is all. I need a break. I was headed home and they sent me here. What am I supposed to do?" He turned back to me. "Sorry if I seem pushy, sir, but this IS a fresh murder. Yeah, you got hit on the noggin, but you're also the only person I can connect to this woman. Wadja call her? Nadia? You're probably the very last person to see her alive. That makes you a prime suspect, whack on the head or not. You could've had a fight with her and she ended up dead. Simple, eh? Happens all the time. Even in the best of families. Someone makes a remark, someone gets a little irritated, someone picks up the nearest heavy object, and I get a late night call."

"She was a friend of mine! A professional colleague. We're here in town for a conference."

"What kind of professional? She's dressed like a hooker."

"She liked to dress flashy," I admitted, "but we're genealogists."

"Oh, yeah?"

"Yeah," I echoed. "And y'know, your tone is pretty damn insulting."

"Yeah, yeah, I know. Suspects have rights, too. That's what's been getting wrong with this country. Too many rights. I can't do my job any more. I got to be polite to murderers like you."

"Now wait just a minute. I'm a victim, not a murderer. She was a friend of mine and we were out looking for a nightcap. Some guy attacked us. That's all there is to it. You got a lot of nerve."

The cop didn't back down a bit. "Look at it from my point of view, sir. I'm really not concerned about your feelings, Mr.... What's your name, anyway?"

"Bones. Benjamin S. Bones." I felt around for my wallet to give him my card. It was still in my pocket. I hadn't been robbed.

"Well, Mr. Bones," he said wagging his head back and forth, "I'm more concerned with finding her killer than worried about offending you. It's a matter of priorities, y'see."

"I'll tell you something, Mr. Detective. My interactions with cops in past cases have all been fairly positive. I try to help where I can. You're making this very difficult. Not me. You." I pointed a shaking finger at him.

"Oh, so you been arrested before, sir?" He probably thought he had me now. "Where? When? What were the charges? Ah... never mind. I'll look you up in the computer."

What a jerk, I thought. This guy is dangerous. He wants his case wrapped up because he's tired, and I'm his first and closest potential perpetrator. The problem is, I'm the other victim. I reminded the cop of that. "Y'know... I'm a victim here, too. I'm lucky I didn't get killed tonight."

"Well, right now you look like a suspect to me. What're you hiding behind that beard? I still think you could'a been fighting with the broad, and..."

This wasn't getting me anywhere. "I don't want to go to the hospital. I want to go to my hotel." I worked myself up to a standing position. I felt rocky. The EMT held me while my sense of balance came back.

"By the way, what did the guy rob you of? Wallet? Credit cards? What?"

I knew that I still had my wallet.

"He didn't get anything from me. And Nadia was already down and probably out cold, so I doubt he got anything from her either."

"That's real interesting," said the detective. "We rarely have a mugging where no one loses nothing." He turned his head up and sniffed at the cool evening air. "I smell a rat."

"That is interesting," I agreed. "Why would a mugger mug people and run away with nothing to show for his effort?"

"Right," he agreed all too enthusiastically. This didn't look good for me. "Dreadlocks, eh? That might or might not be significant. Asheville's a hip kinda town. Lots of dreadlocks around. Men and women both." His eyes seemed to roll a bit. And then he dug into my story again, "You notice any piercings or tattoos around the neck, face, or hands? How about fancy earrings? Maybe a bolt through his nose?"

"You're joking, right?" I couldn't believe this guy. "That's a lot to notice when I was scared out of my wits and Nadia was down on the ground like that." I pointed toward her neatly sheeted body.

He changed course. "You staying at the Asheville Pisgah Hotel? That's where the conference is, right?"

I nodded. "Yes, that's right. I'm in room 635."

"635," he repeated, like he was slotting my room number into a brain compartment. "I'll stop by and see you. I was going to be over there anyway. Gen'ology's a hobby of mine, y'know." He smirked. "Suits my investigative nature."

"Great. I won't look forward to seeing you there." We sure had started out on the wrong feet.

Chapter 2 – 5 P.M. – Free Drinks for All

I'm Ben Bones, Consulting Genealogist and Articulator of Family Skeletons.

In my work, I don't search for personal wealth or acquisition for the sake of mere acquisition. I find the missing dead, people lost in the mists of history, lost amid crumbling documents in old library tomes, and more and more nowadays on the Internet. Where's Great Uncle Lou who moved west to dig for California gold and was never heard from again? Don't worry, I'll find him. In a reasonable time and at reasonable rates, too. That's how I earn my living.

Sounds simple enough, doesn't it? Someone calls, hires my research skills, and off I go to fill in the blanks in their genealogical chart. That's the theory, but it never seems to work out that way.

I've had research jobs where I've been shot at, thrown into the ocean amidst feeding sharks, and I've stood and watched people as they literally killed one another. For what? Greed is always a great motivator, but it's not always the only goad to nefarious action. Maybe I'll uncover a long hidden family secret that the folks who hired me don't want revealed. Everyone has an agenda, and they rarely tell me the full truth about what it is at the start. As I like to say, "A genealogist's life is fraught with danger." Laugh if you will, but I've got the scars to prove it.

This time was supposed to be different. I wasn't on a research job for avaricious maniacs. I was in beautiful Asheville in the western North Carolina mountains attending a genealogical convention. I came to fraternize with other seekers of missing truths in a collegial atmosphere, and had expected a relaxing few days in a mountain hotel amidst like-minded professionals.

But other folks had other ideas, as usual, and guess who found himself in the middle? Still have no idea? I'll give you a hint… yours truly, Ben Bones, Articulator of Family Skeletons.

According to the Internet, Asheville is known to aficionados as "Beer City." It's become famous for its micro-breweries and craft beers, whatever that means. Of course, all that came much later, long after the Vanderbilts had acquired the western North Carolina mountains, constructed the fabled chateau in the woods known to the world as the Biltmore House, and the town itself had blossomed into a vacation haven for the Victorian rich. The town of Hot Springs with its healing baths was only a pleasant forty mile junket north through the forest toward the Tennessee line.

Asheville is regularly listed as one of the "best places" to vacation in or retire to, and consequently the town has grown considerably over recent years. It's still small when compared with Chicago or L.A., but it has its own peculiar ambiance, as the bumper stickers reading "Keep Asheville Weird" attest. It has become haven to many retired folks, young artists of all medias, the tattooing center of the Carolinas, North Carolina's gay and lesbian capital, and a Democratic island in a largely Republican sea. It even boasts a t-shirt from WCQS, the local public radio station, bearing the legend "Welcome to the Cesspool of Sin - Asheville." That was an actual insult that State Senator Jim Forrester from further east had thrown at the town. The cooler people of Asheville jumped on it right away and immortalized the slur.

In short, if you believe the brochures, Asheville is a town that enjoys life, art and music, and for all the problems that any town has, it can laugh at itself, and frequently does. It's a tongue-in-cheek town. I had thought about moving here myself at various times. Still might. Who knows? I'm certainly perceived as odd enough by various folks I meet elsewhere. I'm sure I'd melt virtually unnoticed into the local population.

* * *

Checking into the Asheville Pisgah Hotel had been simple enough. We all know how it goes. Just tell the intern or recent hospitality management graduate working the desk your name and hand them your currently un-maxed credit card, and the job is done. It's all taught in their basic first courses. Oh, and don't forget to smile at the guests and call them "sir" or "ma'am."

Mag-striped key card in hand, I dragged my rolling suitcase with the delicately balanced cardboard box of handouts atop it into the elevator, and rode the faux elegant contrivance a few floors up and a bit closer to heaven. Reaching the sixth floor, I headed down the hall to my room.

Inside room 635, there was nothing unexpected, of course. Surprises were on the agenda for later that evening. The room had all the standard hotel decorations: paint-by-numbers landscapes in fancy gold-anodized stamped aluminum frames, a platform bed, plastic cups in unopenable wrappers, and a sanitized toilet seat with a paper band across it that effectively blocked any basic animal functions.

After spreading my papers out and settling in, it was time to find the conference registration desk and link up with some of my brother and sister genealogists. That was the point of this trip, wasn't it? Professional hobnobbing. That and the tax deductible expenses that we all love. I don't take trips just for fun. Haven't done that for as long as I can remember. If I go somewhere, I always wander over to the local library or genealogy society. Then I can legitimately claim to Uncle Sam that the trip was a research junket.

Leaving my room, I hustled down the five flights to the first floor. I try to avoid elevators whenever possible. My work keeps me sitting at the computer far too much, so if there's any opportunity to move my body around, I take it, except for dancing that is. Going up the stairs with my suitcase and a box full of printed handouts might have tested my stamina, but descending empty-handed was a piece of cake. I knew that I was kidding myself by calling it exercise. I'm pretty clear about that sort of self-delusion.

I followed the Western North Carolina Genealogy Society conference signs around a corner of the lobby to the registration table where several extravagantly dressed young women sat chatting. I went up to the one with a file box close at hand. She was dressed up like for a prom in a floppy off-white dress and huge corsage at her shoulder. Her name tag said "Virginia - WNCGS Staff." I introduced myself.

"Oh, Mr. Bones. Glad you could join us this year. We're all looking forward to hearing about some of your adventures."

"Just call me Ben. I'm not 'mister' anybody."

"All righty, then, Ben," the young lady said with a smile that revealed lots of brilliant white teeth set in plenty of gums and separated in front by a wide diastima. She riffled through the file box in front of her, found my folder, and pulled out a neck hanger with my presenter's credentials in a clear plastic sheath. Handing them to me, she added, "Do you want your entire packet now, or will you pick it up tomorrow morning?"

"Tomorrow will be good enough. But do you happen to have a copy of the schedule that I can stuff into my pocket now for quick reference?"

She took a folded program from a pile to one side and handed it to me.

"That will tell you where tonight's mixer is, but you really don't need a map to find it. It's right around the corner there in Vance-B." She pointed with a needlessly long blazing crimson fingernail. Some sort of an animal gee-gaw had been glued on top of the nail for good measure. "We've provided an open bar for presenters and vendors. Some of our staff will be there, too. And Buck and Vivian, of course." With a playful pout she added, "I have to work registration tonight, but I might could get away later . . ."

"Might see you there then. That's where I'll be." I countered, with no hidden agenda.

"All righty, then," she said again. If that was the cleverness of all her conversation, I'd already had enough. It sure was great being a well-known celebrity, even in the small incestuous world of professional genealogists. Perks appeared unexpectedly here and there, whether you wanted them or not.

I turned and headed for the open bar. That's where my troubles of the evening began.

Ben Bones & the Conventional Murders

Chapter 3 – Evening – The Presenters Meet

Meeting room Vance-B had three solid walls and one of those rubberized folding concertina walls that I could safely assume divided it from Vance-A. It wasn't a tough conclusion to reach. I'd been to conference hotels before. They usually did the most with the least, or at least with the cheapest.

The lighting in Vance-B had been minimized to create a cozy bar-like atmosphere, and Vivian Bradford was right there to greet me as I wandered in through the wide open double door.

Vivian was the wife of WNCGS President Buchanan "Buck" Bradford, and like last year, she handled much of the day-to-day conference administration. It was people like her and their never flagging efforts that made these conferences work. Taking her hand, I made my obeisance.

"Vivian. Great to see you again."

"Hi, Ben. It's so very good to see you again, too. How long has it been?"

Vivian was an unattractive fire-plug of a woman, chunky and only five feet tall, with tightly permed thinning hair of no easily identifiable color. She was dressed in a flowing robe that hid the true outlines of her bulk, and she wore no makeup, perhaps because she realized it wouldn't have helped and was a waste of money. But in spite of all that, she was a gracious and enthusiastic welcoming hostess, a perfect foil to her genealogist husband Buck's glacial academic facade. He was the intellect in the family, while she was the gifted socializer. A functional match, it was, if not "made in heaven," at least made to serve in heaven's anteroom here on earth.

"Vivian. It's good to see you, too. Actually, I think the last time we saw each other was at your conference here last year. That was a great get-together. Your workshop schedule looks like it's dynamite for this year, too."

"We've certainly worked hard enough putting it all together. Can't let our regulars down now, can we?" she said with a big smile. And with me taken care of, she turned to shine her welcoming effulgence on the next arrival.

I looked around the dimly lit hospitality room to see who was there, who was with whom, and to decide whom to greet next.

Standing near the bar with a drink in hand, WNCGS's president, Buchanan "Buck" Bradford was chatting with some genealogical big-wigs. As another guest came through the door, I broke loose from Vivian and headed for the bar myself. Right next to Buck was Carl Heinrich Van Steuben, a noted researcher and something of a genealogical curmudgeon. I wondered what he was up to. He'd figured out how to turn genealogy into cash early in his career and whenever I encountered him, he was invariably working some angle or other.

Standing with them were Dr. Emanuel Whalen, a respected death certificate expert, Theron R. Quince, the acknowledged expert on Southern bastardy bonds, and our Internet research maven, Fanny Quinlan-Bolt. All of them were presenters on the conference program. Even though I was on the program too, I felt I was heading into somewhat rarified air. I took a deep breath and dove in.

As I approached the group at the bar, Buck announced my arrival. "Look who's here. Do you all know Ben Bones?"

Some of the folks nodded vaguely, but one woman grabbed my arm with unexpected force. "I sure do. Let the party begin!"

Nadia Worthington-Lamond was a party looking for a place to happen. Any place and any time would do. She was one of those smiling, good looking, provocatively dressed women who you had to be careful with. Although known as a fun party companion, she was also known as someone who might do anything at all to get what she wanted, and thus, she wasn't to be trusted totally. Still, she was great company if there wasn't any prize in contention.

Nadia was also a highly respected researcher who commanded substantial professional fees for any work she took on. As keynote speaker for tomorrow's conference opening, her remarks would be informative as well as entertaining, and any notes taken should be reconsidered carefully after the conference when more time was available. It would be solid stuff. She knew her genealogy.

Nadia clung to me like I was someone really important to her, but I knew it was just her party persona. We'd had fun together at other conferences, but she wasn't a serious woman in my life, nor was I anyone of continuing importance in hers.

"Guess what," she said to me in a stage whisper. "I got the contract!"

"What? What contract?"

She nodded to a dark suit standing with a scotch on the rocks in one hand, and a lithe young brunette in the other. The girl seemed enthralled.

"That's Benton Filgurst. He's a hot shot with the New York publisher Geneal-Xperts. He came down here looking for someone to handle a big book project. And I got the contract!" she beamed.

"Congratulations," I said, somewhat puzzled, "but this is the first I've heard about it. What's it all about?"

"Ten how-to books on genealogical research over a five year period. $10,000 per, plus royalties. I've made it, Ben. I'm a big shot now. You'd better kowtow."

That was big news all right. A contract with a major genealogical publisher to lead a five year project. She'd earn upwards of $100,000, plus royalties and a huge professional boost.

Attending the conference as a presenter and known genealogical author, I might have even been in the running for the contract. Too bad for me, but I was glad she got it. She'd do a great job. She was an excellent researcher and project manager.

"That's great, Nadia. Come on. Let me buy you a drink," I joshed, steering her toward the free bar. Then I saw the Drambuie on the shelf behind the bartender and I knew I had to be careful. But we did have to celebrate. "Barkeeper," I began, raising a pointing finger.

Nadia and I had a couple of drinks and were happily catching up on our respective doings when Buck interrupted the gathering by tapping his prep school ring on his whiskey glass. The conversational buzz quieted as we all turned in his direction.

"Rumors have started flying around, so I thought this would be a good time to set things straight. Our special guest this year is Benton Filgurst," he nodded toward the suit with the attached brunette. "Benton represents Geneal-Xperts, a publishing house I'm sure you're all quite familiar with." There were nods and mumbles all around. Geneal-Xperts was a major genealogical publisher of research materials, indexes and private vanity books.

"He came down to North Carolina this year to find an editor for a series of genealogical how-to books. I'm happy to announce…, well, maybe I'll let Benton have the honors." He gestured to Filgurst. The suit stepped briskly to where Buck stood, the babe following as if on a tether. Her head bounced as if loosely attached.

"Thanks, Buck." His voice was smooth and deep, rich with overtones, yet measured and safely corporate at the same time. "As Buck said, I came here to sign up an editor." He summoned Nadia to his side with a come-hither hand gesture. "I'm pleased to announce that even before the conference got going, we've made our decision. Nadia Worthington-Lamond here has the job."

It was official. We all applauded politely, though I saw sneers and snarls on some people's faces, undoubtedly people who felt the contract should have been theirs. Who was this Nadia Worthington-Lamond woman anyway? Such a snooty sounding name. There was no satisfying everyone at anytime, so why wouldn't there be some grumbling amongst this competitive intellectual crowd?

Regardless of whatever suppressed personal resentments and animosities might be percolating, we all raised our glasses in salute to the beaming and beautiful Nadia. Good for her, I thought. She'd do a great job and the others could all just go and choke on their jealousy.

The evening wore on and the mixer was entertaining with the open bar for us privileged few, we presenters at the 3rd Annual Western North Carolina Genealogy Society convention. The conference would begin in full tomorrow morning. Over drinks, I renewed some professional acquaintances, caught up on events in my fellow presenters' lives, and made plans for getting together with people over the next few days.

I was feeling pretty positive about things when the mixer finally broke up at 10:30 P.M. I did have one problem, but not a big one, mind you. You see, they had made my first mistake for me by inviting me to an open bar event. The real problem, my second mistake of the evening, started when I spotted the bottle of Drambuie on the shelf behind the server.

Drambuie: that magical scotch syrup that I love altogether too much and that does me in every time it's put in front of me. As they say in AA, "One is too many, and a thousand is never enough." Knowing what might happen, I ordered one anyway. After all, it was a special occasion, wasn't it? The bartender poured a generous dose, and I was off. I got happy, but I didn't get sloppy falling-down drunk or end up on a table in my underwear with a lampshade on my head. At least, I don't think so. But when the party broke up, I felt I needed to clear my head a bit before heading upstairs to my hotel room.

"Hey, Nadia. How about a stroll downtown before calling it quits for the night?"

Nadia Worthington-Lamond was scheduled to kick the conference off as keynote speaker the next morning, though I didn't see how she could handle it with the load of wine she'd been putting away all evening. She'd been celebrating her $100,000 contract with Geneal-Experts. Besides the cash, the professional notoriety was sure to lead to speaking engagements and other lucrative deals. Her genealogical career would be boosted upwards several serious notches.

"Sure, I could use some clean Appalachian mountain air myself. Let's go." She slid a sinuous arm into the crook of mine and off we went, down the hall, through the marbled lobby, and out into downtown Asheville.

I'd been to Asheville before, so I had a clear idea of where to go. I knew where we could get another drink close by the conference hotel before heading back in for the night. We left the hotel and started walking in the refreshing night air. The moon was almost full, its white light spilling into the unelectrified corners of the downtown streets. The refurbished old brick buildings of this mountain town were picturesque in the moonlight, the deep shadows where the light was blocked giving a mysterious air to various alcoves and recessed doorways.

Feeling a bit impish, I decided to show her the reputedly haunted Chicken Alley on the way to the bar for our nightcap. Supposedly, a Dr. Smith had been killed in a barroom fracas in 1902 and he'd refused to go away ever since. There had been numerous sightings, probably by folks coming out of the same bar he'd been killed in after they'd downed a few.

We wandered down Carolina Lane teasing each other and laughing and made the hook turn into Chicken Alley, a brick mews that ran between the backs of two rows of craft shops.

A couple of hours later, I was nursing a concussion headache and Nadia had been driven to the morgue as an honored guest of the city.

Day 2 – Friday

Chapter 4 – Breakfast with a Twist

Walking into the buffet room, I knew I'd be a hit at breakfast, what with my black eye and the rather noticeable baseball sized lump atop my skull. Maybe I should've worn a disguise: oversized dark glasses, a slouch hat, and my collar pulled up. I could have worn a rubber Halloween gorilla mask and looked a good deal better.

It had been less than ten hours since last night's attack, and I wondered how quickly the grapevine news had traveled amongst the attendees. I wasn't surprised that people noticed my condition, but it was strange that no one commented about poor deceased Nadia.

"Wow! What happened to you, Bones? You fall out of bed during the night?"

"Hey, Bones. Walk into a door?"

"Rough night, Ben?"

"Who worked you over, Bones?"

"Cut yourself shaving, Bones?" That comment was way off the mark. It ignored the fact that I've had a beard for years.

Anyway, that's how I was greeted by friends and colleagues the next morning at the breakfast buffet. I have to admit, my usual reasonably pleasant bachelor face was bruised and cut from the whacks I'd received courtesy of our neighborhood mugger yesterday evening. No beauty contests for me today. Maybe an "ugly man" competition. Regardless, I had survived.

The first person to greet me more personally was Vivian Bradford, the WNCGS president's wife. She rushed up to meet me all dithery, as was her normal style.

"Ben! Oh, I'm so glad you're all right. It must have been horrible."

"I'm sure I've been in worse situations, though I can't recall any right at this moment."

She leaned closer, enveloping me in a dense perfumery. She smelled like an extreme cupcake. "Poor Nadia. That poor woman. And on the eve of her professional triumph, too."

I stepped backward a foot into cleaner air for a cleansing breath.

I'm afraid my response was unnecessarily brutal. "Don't mistake the situation, Vivian. She didn't suffer. She was dead when she hit the pavement. That guy killed her with one whack on the head. She never knew what hit her."

Vivian's usual pallor had pinkened considerably. Her eyes were tearing up and I predicted an imminent saline tsunami. Taking further control of the conversation, I shifted her focus.

"Do you want me to sit anywhere special? Is there a presenters' section for breakfast?"

My question turned her mind from the horror of a respected guest's brutal death and gave her something practical to think about, a problem she could actually solve. She pulled herself somewhat back together into her role as the consummate hostess, even if she was thoroughly stressed out.

"No, nowhere special," she whined. "Buck's going to start things off with an announcement about Nadia, but I don't know what he's planning to do for an opening speaker. She was our planned keynote, y'know."

I nodded.

She sighed and wagged her thinly-haired head back and forth slowly. Her forehead wrinkled. "I think he's asked several people for impromptu remarks."

In better moments, I might've taken her arm and sat with her to keep her from falling apart, but I wasn't feeling all that well myself. I probably did have a concussion, as well as looking like I'd just played several games of ice hockey without any protective gear. I wanted to sit quietly and nurse my wounds privately, or as privately as possible in a room full of 200 or more enthusiastic genealogists hungry for intellectual input, autographs from us well-known and not so well-known presenters, or at a minimum, some firsthand news of last night's mayhem.

I grabbed a black coffee and bagel from the buffet table at the side of the room and found a seat unobtrusively off to one side. There was animated conversation all around me, but I didn't want to interact with anyone. I knew I should try to be personable. Many of these people, the nonprofessional enthusiasts, were potential research clients, but I wanted an impenetrable shield around me just then. Who knew what damage I was doing to my reputation as an approachable and charming researcher? Oh, well. That's life. These weren't my best moments. My head still hurt. Leaving my room, I hadn't even stuffed a handful of business cards into my pockets as I usually did for these shindigs. And I wasn't looking forward to giving my 10 A.M. presentation on some of my more hair-raising genealogical adventures. I'd have to add last night to my future lectures.

I sat there feeling sorry for myself, tore a piece of bagel off, and moved to dunk it into my coffee. Guess who wandered into the room. It was Detective Wilbur Franks, my wannabe pal from last night.

Franks scanned the room. He spotted me. There was no way for me to disappear into the woodwork or under my table. I was trapped. He waved a casual hello and turned to the free cut fruits and baked goodies piled up on the serving tables.

When he had a small plastic plate piled high and a brimming cup of black coffee in his other hand, he headed directly toward me, balancing his collection like a circus performer. I noticed he was wearing a conference badge on a hanger around his neck. Could this be an "unofficial" call? He had said he did genealogy, but I doubted his visit was 100% casual. The previous night's corpse had hardly cooled.

"Mind if I join you?"

"Do I really have anything to say about it?" I retorted.

"Look, last night I wasn't at my best. I'd like to apologize for being so rough on you."

That was interesting. Was this a new and far more subtle interrogation technique? Good cop and bad cop all rolled into one neat package?

"I guess I was a bit off myself," I answered. "At least I had the excuse of being bopped on the head with a plumbing fixture." I stuffed a lump of coffee-saturated bagel into my mouth so I wouldn't have to say anything else.

Buck showed up at that moment.

"So what do you think, Bones? You gonna be able to give your 10 o'clock? It's bad enough that we've lost our keynote speaker, but if you don't feel up to it, I understand perfectly." Buck was being solicitous, if only in his dry academic way.

"No, I'm good to go. Wish I'd gotten a bit more sleep, what with the headache and my face hurting... Well, you know how it goes. To protect and serve!" I joked.

"Yes, I do. A genealogist's work is never done," Buck countered.

If that wasn't already our professional mantra, I doubted I'd ever hear a more appropriate one. As genealogists, it seemed that every nugget of info we found started an entire new trail to more and more nuggets, and each needed further investigating. Family history was a rich intellectual mining landscape, a truly bottomless pit.

"I see I'm speaking in the Merrimon Room. You're expecting me to have a big crowd, eh?" I asked.

"Absolutely. Your writings about your adventures are pretty popular as I understand. I've enjoyed several of your articles myself." Mere frippery from the Master Fripperer Himself.

Wilbur Franks butted in. "I thought I'd seen your name before. Now I've got it! Ben Bones. Yeah. I've read your stuff, too. Pretty entertaining. Funny. You get into some tough situations, don't you?"

"To be honest, they were far from entertaining or funny when I was getting kicked around in the middle of things. It was only later, considered in repose, that the humor of the situations showed through along with all the principals' flaws and antics."

"I think I'll come hear you speak," Franks continued. "Good for my investigation, too. Probably give me insights into your personality and all such as that. Might be able to get the cost of this conference reimbursed by my department." Strangely enough, he winked at me.

Oh, no. Another personable cop. I'd had my doubts after last night's confrontation, but maybe I could get along with this guy after all.

I turned back to Buck. "I'm really looking forward to Theron Quince's presentation on bastardy bonds. I've heard about those things, but never had a need to check it out. Interesting historical backgrounding."

"It's fascinating stuff all right. My family, that's us Bradfords, had a bastardy case a few years after the Civil War. People weren't so delicate about illegitimacy back then. Counties were seriously self-protective about having to support the 'outside child' and didn't worry too much about people's feelings," Buck said. "I never looked into it myself. Suppose I should have, being a professional genealogist and all. You might want to go online and search in Buncombe County bond and apprenticeship court records for the Bradford name. The reputed father's name was Dixon Bradford, and he was something of a local rogue and was eventually killed by a jealous husband over in Waynesville in Haywood County. That's the next county to the west. It makes for a sordid but fascinating family story, don't you think?"

"You seem to know a good bit about it even if you haven't done the formal research," I responded.

"Well, just the family stories I heard from uncles and aunts growing up. Y'know how it goes, the shoemaker's kids going barefoot and all."

"It sounds interesting. I'll check it out, after Theron's lecture though, so I know more about what I have to look for."

I got up to get another coffee and bagel over at the buffet table. On the way, I said hello to some folks I knew from other conferences.

Arriving at the buffet, I saw that most of the food had disappeared into the ravenous maws of the attending genealogists, but I was able to "re-vittle" myself.

A bowtie appeared at my side. It was Orville Twitchell, the Director of Local Historical Services at the Georgia Historical Society. I'd met him while on a research job I did in Savannah.

"Mr. Bones, isn't it? How aaarrrrre youuu?"

"Yes, hi. How are things in Savannah? Still at the Historical Society?"

"Of course I'm still there. Best job I've ever had. Suits me terribly. I meet so many interesting people," he said somewhat coyly. "As for Savannah, that Paneta's Crown discovery of yours really stirred things up. Everyone started digging around in their attics for artifacts, but nothing came anywhere near close to that. Things quieted down after you left town."

"Well, Orville . . . I can call you that, can't I?"

"Oh, call me anything you want, dear boy. Just be sure to call." He painted this invitation with his broadest personal brush.

"Thanks again for your help when I was in Savannah. I couldn't have done it without you." And with that I headed back toward my table and the waiting bloodhound, Detective Franks.

On the way, I spotted Vivian Bradford on the other side of the room. She was talking animatedly with one of the wait staff, a tan-complected young fellow wearing one of those colorful, baggy, knit hats that Rasta folk hide their dreadlocks under. Hotel dress policy, I guessed. Asheville might be a wild and trendy place but business was business after all, and the hotel didn't want to alienate the guests. Not too much anyway.

Back at my table, I pointed the guy out to Franks. "Do you think…?"

"I told you last night… this town has more dreadlocks than they've got in Jamaica. You see those guys all over the place. Women, too. It's an Asheville kinda thing."

"Well, I was just wondering. Why do you think Vivian is talking to him?"

"She's handling all the conference admin details, isn't she? Probably complaining about the service or ordering more bagels for all these vultures." He gestured with an open hand to the genealogical folks scattered about the room. We watched them enthusiastically chowing down.

Still, the guy looked vaguely familiar. Nah. He couldn't have anything to do with last night's misadventure. No one would be dumb enough to pull something like that in the evening and then re-enter the lion's den the next morning.

Chapter 5 – A Keyless Keynote

After breakfast, I followed the shuffling crowd to the plenary session in Asheville Pisgah Hotel's Merrimon Room. What would the news of Nadia's death do to the conference? A vibrant and respected genealogist, she was supposed to be our keynote speaker this morning. Her unexpected and violent death couldn't help but throw a malignant shadow over the proceedings.

Buchanan "Buck" Bradford was himself known as an unflappable and precise researcher who never missed a deadline, and his presidency of the Western North Carolina Genealogy Society followed his personal style. His trains ran on time. Buck called the Plenary Session to order at exactly 9 A.M.

I didn't envy our fearless leader his task of informing the assembled genealogists about last night's horror. Nadia was quite well known, not only as a tireless and thorough researcher, but as a friend to many of us. I wondered whom Buck had recruited on such short notice to fill in as keynote speaker.

He dragged himself unenthusiastically to the rostrum and looked around. It was definitely not his best moment. He'd make the televised news that night though.

"Rumors are flying all around about what happened last night downtown. I might as well simply say it straight out. Nadia Worthington-Lamond, our illustrious keynote speaker and winner of the Geneal-Xperts book contract, was killed last night in the street by a mugger."

The air seemed to rush out of the room. Even knowing what was coming and as quiet and attentive as we had all been before Buck's announcement, it was nothing compared to the interstellar vacuum that now gripped us. Two hundred souls were unable to catch their breath for the sheer shock of the news.

Ben Bones & the Conventional Murders

Buck looked us over bleakly, seeming to be at a loss for what to do next. It was very uncharacteristic for him.

"Can you tell us exactly what happened?" someone yelled out.

"Where'd it happen?" another voice, a woman's, called.

Buck looked over at me where I sat, cocked his head and raised an eyebrow. I assumed he wanted some help. Reluctantly, I stood and turned to the group. I wasn't very good with eulogies. I'd given them up after the funerals of my murdered wife Sarah and our unborn baby.

I stood there for a few seconds trying to figure out something to say, anything really, something that might make some sense of the random death that had kicked our conference off.

"What happened, Bones? Were you there?"

I spotted Detective Franks leaning against the wall toward the back of the room. He'd undoubtedly be making notes on whatever I said.

I looked the crowd over. Some were old friends and colleagues. Many were strangers to me. They ran the cultural gamut from your basic housewives and staid banker-looking types right across the spectrum to several tattooed and pierced teenagers. There were even a few dreadlocked Rastas in the house. No one was eating. No one was fussing with their make-up. No one was riffling through their briefcase papers. Their eyes were fixed on me like a cat's on a soon-to-be-victim fledgling bird that had fallen from the nest. Even in the normally flat room lighting, I felt spotlighted. Feeling as awkward as I'd ever felt before in my life, I cleared my throat and dove in.

"Well," I began tentatively, "There isn't much to say. Nadia and I went out for a walk after the hospitality bar closed..." I took a deep breath, "...and we were jumped by some guy waving a piece of pipe around. I ended up on the ground with my face cut up a bit as you can see, and when I woke up, the EMT told me Nadia was dead. That's really all I know," I said with a shrug, my hands spread out to the sides.

I returned to my seat feeling pretty well bummed out. Definitely not my usual energetic self. Wilbur Franks came over and sat down next to me.

"You sounded pretty credible there, Bones. I have to admit I'm starting to believe your story."

"Thanks," I muttered somewhat sarcastically, not really giving the least concern to whether he believed me or not. My heart hurt as well as my head. And it wasn't something I needed to see a cardiologist about either. Maybe a grief counselor. Or was I feeling a survivor's guilt?

"You're welcome," he said. "But I still have a murder to solve. If you think of anything else that might be useful, be sure to let me know."

"Sure. But I've told you everything already." There was nothing more to it.

***

People come to conventions and professional conferences for a variety of reasons. Professional development is big: learning the latest research techniques and tools, discovering new helpful software, gathering lists of recently established websites, learning how to track wives with their ever-changing last names. And of course, there were two of my favorite topics: how to handle difficult clients, and how to wring cash from deadbeats. Lots of tax-deductable expenses can pile up over a weekend's learning experience, too. Hang on to all your receipts. And be sure to pick up any others you see discarded on the floor.

Another reason to attend is for the sheer joy of mingling with like-minded people, other genealogy geeks like ourselves. As genealogists, we tend to work in isolation. We used to hang out in library stacks digging through boxed archives of crumbling documents. Of course, nowadays we can glean much the same information online. The work doesn't entail as much travel, but we still find ourselves working alone, perhaps at home, with only our blues CDs and a tempting refrigerator for company. It's all too easy to put on a few pounds in the bargain.

No one goes to a convention for the murders.

And yet, there we all sat, perhaps two hundred kindred souls, sitting in a room with no air in it, the inescapable pall of death draped over us, shading us from the sun's light and postponing our genealogical enlightenment.

Genealogists seek death. But we're not looking for deaths in the present. We seek the long departed and the evidence trails they've left behind. And the further back from the present, the better. We want to document their footprints through time and geography. We want proof of the family stories, proof in the form of census and court records, wills and codicils, immigration and voting records, city directories and professional journals, or even the daily newspapers announcing births, weddings, and divorces. All these comprise our hunting grounds.

But when we're confronted with an immediate and unexpected death, the death of a loved one, a friend, a professional colleague, we don't react as academics. In spite of what cynics might think, genealogists are human, too. We have feelings, we have visceral reactions, we feel hunger, pain, loss. And, just like normal human beings, we have to deal with the grief for however long and at whatever intensity it lasts.

For me, Nadia had been a friend. Over the years we'd shared a good many drinks together, lots of laughs, and a few intimate moments, too, I have to admit. But this was the morning after, and I felt the loss deeply. And there was something else here, too. I think it was guilt. If I hadn't suggested we go downtown for a nightcap, she'd be standing at the podium right now regaling us with insights that would grow us all to be more competent seekers. Instead, well…

Buck broke into my reverie. "Some of you know that Nadia had been named to head a substantial multi-book project for Geneal-Xperts, one of the top genealogical publishing houses. That position of lead editor is now open again." He nodded to a distinguished-looking fellow who stood off to the side in a tweed jacket despite the heat, a coffee cup in one hand. "Benton Filgurst of Geneal-Xperts is with us this weekend, and it looks like the competition for the contract will be restarted, though not from scratch. There's what we call a 'short list' of contenders. Mr. Filgurst would like to meet with the following people right after this session: Olivia Trueblood, Cornelius Reese, Faith Willoughby, Ben Bones, Carl Van Steuben, and Theron Quince. I'll be there, and anyone else who's interested can attend, too. It's an open session."

I knew a few of those named personally, others only by reputation. And I was surprised that I had made the list. Surprised and honored. Maybe I was more respected professionally than I had thought. Probably fallout from the entertaining articles I wrote about the various genealogical puzzles I've dealt with over time, not to mention the crazy people I've met through my work.

Buck closed the session with a few announcements about room changes and other administrivia. He hadn't gotten another speaker to fill the gap after all. There was lots of mumbling as the session broke up and people began to wander about aimlessly to await the first formal presentations. I snatched up my laptop bag and joined the group of contract candidates gathering at the front of the room.

Ben Bones & the Conventional Murders

Chapter 6 – The Contract

Buck and Benton herded the short list group of us out of the Merrimon Room and down the hall to a board room with a large mahogany table surrounded by high-backed executive chairs. In addition to the five names that had been called, Vivian was there, as was the former president of the society, Antigone Killian-Groome, a disheveled, semi-inebriated, semi-retired battle-axe. She came clutching a large mug that I doubted held only coffee. She was notorious for beginning her day's imbibing with a breakfast cocktail. This one looked like a triple.

Detective Wilbur Franks tagged along, too, probably to see who might have had a motive to knock Nadia off. Wilbur was a cop, after all. In that, he was a trained paranoid. I'd met his type before. But his was paranoia with a weird angle to it. He wasn't paranoid for himself. Instead, he studied other people's paranoia to see what might motivate them to cross the lines drawn in society's sand. So he hung in the background soaking in everything anyone said, anything anyone did, odd looks people gave, the squint of an eye here, the wrinkled brow there, the rising volume of heated voices in contention. That was the artist's palette from which he painted his pictures of guilt or innocence.

Buck turned the meeting over to Filgurst right away.

"Welcome to you all. I know some of you," he nodded to me, to Theron, to Carl and Olivia." He looked directly at Antigone and said, "I'm sorry, ma'am, but who are you?"

Antigone took an elbow from Faith Willoughby standing next to her. "Eh?"

"Ma'am, who are you?"

"Oh, I'm Antigone Killian-Groome. Maybe you heard of me. I'm sort of a legend with this crowd." She gestured toward the others with an extremely loose hand. "I used to be president of this outfit, but I turned it over to Buck there. Too much work. It interfered with my breakfast Bloody Maries."

"That's quite a recommendation," Filgurst responded. He shook his head in wonder.

Antigone continued in her raw whiskey voice, "By the way, I don't want the job. I just came to see the fistfight between the contenders."

"I prefer the term candidates," Filgurst turned away from Antigone's humorless jibe and toward Cornie Reese. "And you, sir?"

"I'm Cornelius Reese." Cornie answered precisely, drawing up to his full height of 5 foot, 2 inches. He straightened his tie a la Rodney Dangerfield. "I do freelance genealogical research, like some of the others, but much more precisely. I am thus eminently qualified for the editorship, far more than some of these other so-called candidates." He wagged a pointing finger at his perceived competitors.

A dark murmur swept through our small group. Theron's face reddened.

"Yep," Theron agreed. "If you need an *i* dotted or a *t* crossed, Cornie's the one to see. Hey, Cornie, did you get that bumper sticker I recommended, 'Precision Ancestoring?'"

Cornie waved him off. "Aaahhh!"

Filgurst took control again. "Okay. Let me tell you about our project. Genealogy has grown so large as a hobby in the USA that we've decided it's time for us to produce a series of books on genealogy basics for the mass market. We envision 10 books to be done over a 5-year time span. The person we hire to lead the project, who was supposed to be Nadia, will have full editorial control, and can either write the books him or herself, or hire help as needed and compile from different sources. Each book is worth a $10,000 fee for the editor, to spend as you see fit, to purchase repro rights to pictures, articles, whatever. That'll be paid in increments as follows: $3,000 at the start of each book, another $3,000 upon submission of the manuscript, and a final $4,000 upon approval. Plus, once we're done, you'll receive our standard royalty as long as the books are in print. We fully expect your professional reputation to soar with each volume. Geneal-

Xperts is fully behind this and we're sure of substantial sales over the course of time.

"We're looking for someone with a name that's known at least a bit, someone who has a few years of genealogical research experience, excellent writing and editing skills, and can manage a large project. Perhaps most important, we want someone who doesn't miss deadlines. If you don't satisfy those basic criteria, please leave the room. You're not a viable candidate."

There was a bit of muttering, but no one left. People were probably too busy calculating how $100,000 would affect their lives.

Filgurst went on. "I believe I have contact information for most of you. If your name wasn't called at the earlier session, please give me that information now." He waved a yellow pad at us, then flipped it onto the conference table so it slid to the closest person. "I'd also like to receive a resumé from each of you. If you've got a printed copy with you, that's great. If not, email me one at your first opportunity. I plan to make a decision before we all leave on Sunday."

Carl Van Steuben stood up from his chair at the far end of the conference table. "My qualifications are known to everyone. You might as well have me sign a contract before Sunday and save yourself some time."

Olivia Trueblood weighed in at that. "Oh, shut up, Carl. You're a pompous ass and everyone knows it, including yourself."

Carl's face reddened. "Don't get me started, Olive."

"That's 'Olivia,' you ignorant pig," she threw back.

"All right, that's enough of that," Filgurst groped for control. "We'll do this in a civilized way or not at all. I have the final say. So far, it looks like some of you would be hard to work with. That doesn't help your candidacy." He looked everyone in the face, one after another. "You've been convened here because you're all academically qualified. Right now, I'm not so sure about your human characteristics and your ability to work on a team."

It was quiet enough in the room to hear everyone's mental gears grinding out the numbers. To a struggling genealogist, even someone with a well-earned reputation and steady referrals, this project was a lifetime's dream come true. $100,000, a major professional reputation, royalties for years to come, well-paid speaking engagements. I wondered if that was enough motive to interest Detective Franks. I should think it would be enough for anyone. People have committed far more heinous crimes than a late night mugging for a good deal less than that.

Chapter 7 – Bones Articulates

A bit before my 10 A.M. lecture, I entered the Merrimon Room to prepare for my talk. I wanted to check the lighting and get a feel for the room from the speaker's podium. An analog wall clock on the back wall counted the minutes off until starting time.

At first a trickle, then more and more people came in and found places to sit. I recognized a few faces of other presenters in the crowd, as well as my new shadow, Asheville Detective Wilbur Franks, true to his word. By the time I began, there were about 45 people in the audience.

I don't want to repeat the entire text of my talk, but I'll give you a bit. The first thing people usually ask is how we professional genealogists get started in the field. I told about my life-long interest in history, how my parents were practical sorts, and that they'd encouraged me to go for a profession.

"I couldn't stand the idea of practicing medicine. I mean, it was interesting in a way, but the thought of cutting through a living person's skin on purpose for any reason, even to help them out in the long run, appalled me. And hospital aromas had always put me off.

"Law seemed to be deadly dull, at least the lawyers I'd met were, so I decided against either of those trades. Being pretty good in math, I chose accounting, and a few years later I was a junior accountant working in a tiny padded Dilbert cubicle in a mega-corporation that didn't believe in windows. Maybe they were afraid that the boredom would drive the workers to leap out.

"I hadn't been seeking a life of danger and adventure, but accounting was the absolute opposite by definition. I'd become a bean counter, and I learned to hate it. I was bored stiff, so I started looking around for something else to do.

"A friend started digging around in her family's history and asked me for some help. The problems intrigued me. I found the research fascinating, and I discovered a link to a lost relative who had invented a widely used industrial process worth millions and then died intestate. They were able to cash in and the family rewarded me with a fat finder's fee check.

"So basically, it was curiosity and cash that motivated me into genealogical consulting. Not that I'm getting rich. I make my bills every month, and I'm not in debt, but that's about it."

I didn't know if I had my audience enthralled or was boring them stiff, but I plowed on.

"There have been dangerous assignments, too. You wouldn't think so, not in genealogy. A genealogist's life is supposed to be spent in libraries or at the computer creating lineage charts and reports. But that's not where the danger lies in this profession. Believe me, there's more danger in my life than an occasional paper cut."

Several people straightened up in their seats. This was what they'd come for: the blood and guts of genealogy.

"Just as in any line of work, it's the people you meet who provide the variables, the interesting wrinkles, and yes, the danger, mayhem, and horror, too. You see, sometimes people hire me for reasons that seem clearly stated, but many times they have another hidden agenda that I don't find out about until I'm deep in a hole digging out information.

"Let me tell you about a case I call 'The Deadly Descendants.' At the beginning, it sounded like a perfectly simple job. I'd planned to only spend a few days poking around in old property and birth records to build a chart of a deceased husband's early family. But it wasn't that easy. I ended up having my car run off the road, and in the end, uncovering a serial killer. The killer tried to get me, too, but failed. Failed, yes," I paused for effect, "though not by much. That was the most exciting part of the case, but the interesting parts were discovering the hidden history of parenticide murders in the family, finding a missing sibling, and uncloaking a secret bigamist. I learned a lot about human nature on that job.

"One time I was hired to find a missing family artifact. That was the case I call 'The Search for Paneta's Crown.' The father, who held the artifact in trust for the family, died without revealing what the artifact was or where it was hidden. His three adult children each wanted it for themselves, but via the rule of primogeniture, a long standing medieval tradition the family had brought over from Italy, the eldest son was supposed to receive The Crown and hold it in trust for following generations. Needless to say, they fought viciously for it, and guess who was caught in the middle. I got tossed into the ocean for a swim with frenzied sharks off Savannah, Georgia on that trip, and was eye witness to a couple of murders. It wasn't at all what I'd call a dull and routine research job.

"I figured out pretty quickly that although genealogy was a fascinating profession for focused academics, the real interest was in the people, whether living or long dead, whom I encountered. Ours is a human interest job, and it suits me perfectly. If you decide it's the profession for you, don't expect to make a lot of money, except maybe the person who leaves this conference with the $100,000 book contract that's up for grabs, but you'll meet interesting folks and see places and things you never expected to encounter in your lifetime. I guarantee that."

It's tough to read an audience and sometimes I don't know when to quit. But no one had left the room, and no one had fallen asleep, so I figured my presentation was interesting enough.

"I've got a research job coming up in Virginia that involves claiming a Civil War pension for the warrior's descendants. That'll be interesting, and it'll teach me a great deal about that period of American history. I'll be starting on that after I leave this conference. I'm sure there'll be pitfalls along the way, but how bad can the situation get? It's only about a long delayed pension. It's not like there's a fortune at stake for people to fight over, and it will probably turn out to be another fairly simple research job."

That was it for my prepared comments. I opened the floor up for questions, which was how I preferred to spend most of my allotted time anyway. If I gave a few clever answers, I might get a good review and be invited back next year.

"I see a hand in the back there. Do you have a question?"

A tall, stringy fellow in ill-fitting clothes that looked like they'd been his grandfather's stood and asked, "I want to become a professional genealogist. How should I prepare?"

"Are you curious? Are you determined? Are you a creative problem solver? All those things are important. I also recommend that you study human psychology. Find out how people work and what motivates them. That's where your biggest problems will be. Finding family information is only the technical part."

A woman in a flowery dress waved her hand wildly.

"Yes, ma'am . . ."

"I'm new to all this," she drawled. "My sister dragged me over here, but it seems pretty interesting. What all do I need to get started searching for my family's history?" She plunked back down next to a woman who was obviously related, if facial similarity and body type were reliable measures.

"Get hold of a genealogy charting program. There are plenty of them out there, including some free ones. I use a program called 'Body Count' myself. Try a few different programs and find one that you understand and are comfortable with.

"Early on in your research, search out all the old-timers in the family and tape record their family stories. Every family has secrets, too, and if you can get someone to reveal why Aunt Regina was sent to Chicago for several years and then returned to the family's home ground to live a spinster's life . . . well, you might have something really juicy to write about.

"There's usually someone in the family who's already been doing family genealogy. Remember crazy old Aunt Cecilia who everyone laughed at? She brought shoe boxes full of faded photographs to family gatherings and bothered everyone trying to put names on the people in them. Find her or her descendants and get hold of those boxes. They're full of family treasure.

"And of course, join your local genealogy society or the society in the area the family lived. Nowadays, we tend to scatter all over the country, but in the old days, families stuck close together. The regulars at the local society can lead you through the basics of genealogical searching. They're genuine subject matter experts and their goal is to spread the genealogical gospel. Take advantage of their knowledge and helpfulness."

I scanned the room for more raised hands. Detective Franks had his hand up.

"Yes, Detective. What have you got for me?"

Heads jerked around to see who "Detective" might be. There were a few whispered comments to neighboring attendees. I saw one guy slink down in his seat a bit, as if he suddenly didn't want to be noticed.

Franks stood. Even in his off-duty clothes, he reeked of "cop." I don't know what it is about those guys. Perhaps it's a professional demeanor that's impossible for them to shed. Maybe it's the suspicion they view everyone with. But it's there, and easy enough to spot.

"Do you ever find evidence of crimes in the past? What do you do with that information?" he boomed out. A cop query for sure. There were a few more mumbles in the audience.

"An interesting question. Yes, there are times when the family's darkest secret is a murder or intra-family theft. I remember once finding an embezzlement from an estate. One of the lawyer nephews had been named to handle the probate, but greed got the better of him. He wasn't a named beneficiary, but by the time the probate was over, he'd eaten most of the assets up in legal fees and what he called administrative costs. It wasn't labeled embezzlement outright, but that's what it was. He wasn't charged with a crime because it looked legitimate. He hadn't been one of the popular family members to begin with, but that finished him off and severed his relations with the rest of the family.

"And there's an occasional family murder or other mayhem. Maybe a domestic restraining order on a spouse or a custody battle complete with an interstate child abduction. I found a bigamist once. It wasn't what I was looking for, but there it was."

Franks still stood, his head nodding. He had enjoyed that. Forensic genealogy. It was something he could thoroughly enjoy.

"Crime in the family creates other problems, too. One friend of mine refused to get involved in research on his own family because he saw it as a hopeless endeavor from the start. His rural family for several generations back had been a tangle of bootleggers and petty thieves, like the Timpson clan in John Mortimer's Rumpole stories. Normally, arrest records can provide good historical information, but he said there were scads of arrests in those generations, and every time someone was arrested, they'd give a fictitious name. He thought that the trails would be so hard to follow that he didn't even want to begin. I thought it would be a great project to take on."

That got a big laugh from the crowd. Maybe some of them could relate to that sort of behavior.

Another hand went up. Oh, no. It was Flavia "Gammie" Gamitter again, a woman who seemed to materialize wherever I happened to go. It was like being stalked by an overweight, toothless predator caricature who only wanted a friendly scratch behind the ears. And the cloud of perfume that thickened the air around her! Whew!

"Yes, Gammie. What have you got for me?"

She shuddered with anticipation. "I was wondering what you were doing for dinner tonight. I thought we might..." she began shamelessly. There were snickers from the crowd.

"Sorry, Gammie, but I've got plans. Genealogy meetings. That sort of thing."

"Maybe some other time… tomorrow?"

I shook my head negatively. We'd been through this before at other conventions and workshops. She was tenacious, if nothing else, but she wasn't my type. Perhaps not anyone's. I felt bad for her, but it was never going to happen.

"I see that we're about out of time. I'll be happy to talk to anyone during the conference. Catch me in the hall or wherever. This is my meat and potatoes. Just try to shut me up," I challenged. "And don't forget to check out my website: benbones.com."

I got a short round of applause, and people began to mill around. It was time for me to go hear Theron Quince's presentation on bastardy bonds. After I'd learned something on the topic and grabbed a quick lunch, I planned to spend the rest of the afternoon back in my room pecking away at my laptop looking into Buck Bradford's family as he'd suggested that morning.

Chapter 8 – The Other – #1

Where was that boy? He was never around when you wanted him. Been like that all his life. But at least he had finally found a responsible hotel job that kept him from running around all crazy. It suits his ADHD personality.

This time he blew it for us though, and for me in particular. And now they're on to him. I know that detective. They're going to put it all together and they're going to catch him for killing that poor woman.

And when they get him, he's gonna blab because he's a young fool, and then they'll get to me. It will all have been for nothing. All my planning, all my work: the conference, getting Geneal-Xperts to come with that big, fat contract. No chance for Buck getting it after that.

The boy's got to go away for a while. Not for long. Just until the conference is over. That'll be enough. That will do it. Just until they all go home. Then things will settle back down to normal again and everything will be all right.

If that boy had just thought about what he was doing. Well, I can't really blame him for the woman's death. How could he know that he'd kill her? He simply hit her too hard. Maybe she had a soft skull.

But it sure did take her out of the picture and open the competition up again. Not at all the way I'd planned, but successful beyond my initial thinking.

I've got to find him, talk to him, convince him to leave town. Maybe he's in that kitchenware stocking area.

Ah, there he is.

"Ollie! Ollie, come here for a minute."

Chapter 9 – Bastardy Bonds Revealed

Just before 11 that morning, I worked my way through an enthused crowd and entered the Vance-B meeting room for Theron Quince's lecture on bastardy bonds.

I didn't know exactly what to expect. I'd met Quince at other genealogical events, and I knew he was the recognized expert on this topic, as well as other equally fascinating and arcane subjects. We'd been thrown together on several other occasions, and I'd always left with the feeling of having met a true genealogy geek, a guy who was totally committed to his academic side, always right about his topics, and who had a negligible personality to go along with his erudition. He was the kind of genealogist a "normal" person might expect to meet, not a personable, good-looking, even if cynical, widower like myself.

But I had come to the lecture in a quest for some of that arcane knowledge. If I'd wanted pure entertainment, I could've gone across town to one of the local comedy clubs.

I found a seat near the end of a row and pulled out my iPad to take notes.

"Hi, Ben."

Oh, no. It was Flavia Gamitter again. I couldn't shake her. At this point, it seemed her crush on me was determining the lectures she attended. She plopped her bulk down in a seat directly behind me and loomed over my shoulder. I thought I smelled wine from the plastic cup in her hand. It mixed with her make-up aromas and heavy perfume miasma to form a viscous atmosphere around her. I was reminded of the cloud that surrounded the Pigpen character in Charles Schultz' *Peanuts* cartoon strip.

"Hi, Gammie," I responded unenthusiastically. I didn't want to be rude, but I had to figure out a way to stop her from following me around. At the moment there were people seated on both sides of me and I couldn't easily get away.

"It's so good to see you again, Ben. And I loved your lecture this morning. Did you notice that I was there? I heard every word," she rattled on without taking a breath.

"Yes, I saw you. And I heard you, too. You asked me a question. Don't you remember?"

"Oh, yeah," she giggled. "I did, didn't I?" She shrugged her broad shoulders coquettishly. "I guess I forgot. What was the question?"

"I don't remember, Gammie. But right now I need to pay attention to this lecture, if you don't mind."

"Oh," she mumbled, and she slid backwards into her seat.

After that brief exchange, the lecture proceeded in a more predictable manner. There was the introduction of "our highly regarded expert, Theron R. Quince," followed by a parenthetical on where the bathrooms and water fountains were located. And then Theron launched himself. Rather, he got off to a crawling start and proceeded to slow down from there. It was a good bit less than inspiring. You really had to be fascinated by bastardy bonds, and perhaps even be a closet bastardy bond geek to stay awake. Needless to say, I was wide-eyed.

Looking around the room, I saw I was one of about fifteen people who were aching to hear about bastardy bonds in the American South. There was only one other lecture being given in the same time slot: *Etiquette for Genealogists,* in Vance-A next door. I could hear some mumbling through the unfolded accordion wall, but not enough to make sense of it. Maybe almost everyone had gone out to lunch downtown and forgotten to come back to the conference. So much for dedication to our craft.

Theron got through his prepared material in short order. There wasn't much to it. He talked a bit about the historical basis for the bonds, how they derived from old English law that followed settlers to the early Colonies, and the process counties went through to establish paternity in questionable situations. Most interesting were the examples he projected on screen of actual court documents he'd photographed at the North Carolina State Archives in Raleigh. The spelling in them was atrocious to my officious grammatical eye, but in those early days, the mid-1800's, literacy wasn't as widespread as it is today and there was little standardization in spelling. We had a few good laughs at some of the idiosyncrasies. I was reminded of a reported quote from Mark Twain: "Anyone who can only think of one way to spell a word obviously lacks imagination."

And of course there was a "Q and A" session at the end of his prepared lecture.

A woman in the last row of seats called out in a husky voice. "Do we have to go to the State Archives to search for these documents?" I recognized Antigone Killian-Groome's smoker's rasp and the slur from her breakfast imbibing. It amazed me that she could think straight enough to pay attention to a lecture and then come up with a coherent and relevant question. A truly remarkable woman, not to mention a high-functioning alcoholic.

"Much of this material is beginning to appear online. It's not like the good old days," Theron tried to joke. There was something about his personality, or lack of it, that killed the jest and dropped it to the floor like a dead fish attempting to catch its watery breath. He ploughed on though, absorbed in his topic and oblivious to the lack of audience response.

"Visit your favorite genealogical search sites and start digging. You're bound to come up with something. If nothing else, it'll give you good reason to visit Raleigh at a later date." I was planning to go online myself after he finished and I'd had a bite of lunch.

"There's a handout to go along with my lecture. The conference staff has left a pile of them near the door. Please pick one up as you leave."

I did.

***

Wandering back out into the crowded convention hallway, it felt good to be able to take a deep breath of clean North Carolina mountain air after spending an hour and a half submerged in the cloying cloud that surrounded Gammie. I'll grant that I'm still young enough to be eligible, and I may not be rich, although I am self-supporting, but what was the special magic that attracted ardent fans like Gammie into my orbit? Maybe they don't read me for the "damaged goods" that I am.

Why do I say that? Because of the crippling relationship trauma I'd lived through some years ago. Sarah had been my childhood sweetheart all the way back to fourth grade. Eventually we married, and she was going to be my future. She was the love of my life, as people are fond of saying. Unfortunately, life made a sudden U-turn on me about eight years ago when my wife and unborn child were killed in a drive-by shooting. My glorious plan for the future became a bleak unrealizable dream because some jerk driving a stolen car had pulled a trigger. What was he trying to prove? And to whom? We never found him and we never discovered why. All I had left was the resulting wreck of my planned life.

In any event, I was suddenly free in lots of unintended ways, except that I didn't feel free to get involved in another relationship. Sarah had been the one for me, and that was still true so many years later. I felt it would have been disloyal of me.

Not that I don't like girls, mind you. I had all the right excuses. It hadn't been long enough since Sarah was killed. I hadn't healed yet. That relationships demanded too much time, too much energy, too much money . . . you get the idea.

But if I talked to a shrink, she'd probably be able to nail me with the one thing I avoided admitting to myself for a long time, even though I knew it was there: that I was wary about making another commitment, afraid it would only be snatched away from me again. I was plain old scared.

Knowledge may be power, but self-knowledge isn't freedom, no matter what people say. It's just the beginning of a haunting that doesn't feel like it'll ever quit.

But my personal ghosts don't stand in the way of my professional genealogical life as Ben Bones, Articulator of Family Skeletons and Finder of the Unfindable. That had become my real life, and it's where I wanted to live, amongst other people's deceased relations. Not my own.

Chapter 10 – A Face in the Crowd

Asheville is a great restaurant town. The variety of eating places is extraordinary. You can have your choice of Japanese, Thai, Indian, Italian, Latin, traditional Southern BBQ, or even an occasional steak house. One neighborhood bar even served up imported Ethiopian fare every Tuesday evening.

One reason for all these choices is that the local community college, Asheville-Buncombe Technical Community College, has a well-respected culinary program. Graduates are qualified to go anywhere to pursue their careers, but the quirkiness of Asheville's hip culture and the magic of the Appalachian mountains hold many of them in town after graduation. Some go to work for established restaurants. A few, the more adventurous or perhaps the trust fund babies, start their own small places. Many of these young entrepreneurs fail, but some succeed wildly because of their innovative menus or simply because of their excellent food. Clever décor, of which there's plenty, doesn't fool anyone; it's the food that counts.

I'm something of a "foodie" myself. Since being forced back into bachelorhood by my life circumstances, I've learned that in order to eat well, I had to learn to cook well. Over time, that's what I did, particularly in a variety of Oriental styles. Simply put, I learned to cook because I like to eat.

But on this day, after last night's excitement, the soreness I still felt from the beating I'd taken and the stimulation of the conference, I wasn't in the mood for exotic cuisine artistically prepared and served up with a lonely sprig of parsley or shiso leaf on the side. I wasn't up to venturing out into the city for a gourmet meal. A simple club sandwich in the hotel's café would satisfy me perfectly, and without too much effort or expense on my part.

I ran into Detective Franks unexpectedly in the hall and we headed for the hotel's café. It looked like I was stuck with him for the weekend. His personal interest in his family's genealogy notwithstanding, I was a "person of interest" in his hottest case. Still, he seemed like a sharp enough fellow. If I paid attention, I might learn a few things from him before saying a heartfelt goodbye on Sunday when the conference ended.

"Let's get a small table," I said. "There's a woman following me around and I don't want to leave her an opening to join us."

Franks cackled sardonically out of one side of his mouth. "So you got a girlfriend already? Since last night, I mean?"

"I already told you that Nadia was a professional colleague, not a girlfriend. How many times do you want to hear it?"

He pulled back and put his hands up in a ward off gesture. "Yeah, yeah, I heard you clear enough the first time. I'm just jerking your chain a little."

"Well, cut it out. This woman is a real pain. I try to avoid her, but she shows up everywhere I go. It's like having an extra shadow."

We found a circular two person table near a floor-to-ceiling window that looked out on Asheville's cityscape in one direction and back into the hotel lobby in the other.

The city was a mix of new and old architecture, complete with colorful wall murals and remarkably colorful citizens going about purposefully. Tourists were easy to spot, too, wearing their crisply pressed madras shorts, with children in tow and expensive digital cameras draped around their necks on Nikon or Canon straps. It was like a uniform that the local citizenry wasn't permitted to copy.

Locals, on the other hand, were an eclectic mix of styles, everything from fashionably torn camo T-shirts and colorful Rasta hats to the standard dark blue banker's banality and everything in between. Lots of facial piercings, too, and I'd bet those folks were pierced in places that weren't open to public viewing as well. Other southern towns had a church or two on every corner. Asheville sported a tattoo or piercing parlor and one or two craft beer joints on every block. I'd seen a bumper sticker that said "Keep Asheville Weird." They meant it.

A young waitress in dreadlocks down to her butt, fur-topped boots up to her knees, and perhaps the shortest polka dot skirt I'd ever seen or even imagined came over with water glasses and menus. We watched her silently. Without a smile or a word, she turned and went off to other duties.

"Y'see? Dreadlocks. They're everywhere," said Franks, his hands spread in an expansive explanatory gesture. "It might be a clue and it might not. There's no telling at this stage."

I had to agree. "Yeah. I see what you mean. There seem to be far more dreadlocks per capita here than in Atlanta."

"That's where you're living?" He couldn't resist doing his detective thing.

"Outside of Atlanta actually. In a small town called Austell just west of the city. It's what they call a 'bedroom community' for Atlanta itself. It's cheaper and nowhere's near as fancy as the north side of Atlanta, but it suits me." I took a sip of water and flipped my menu open. "But I'm looking to relocate somewhere smaller than the metro Atlanta area. Much of my work is online now or in exotic locations where my clients live. The ride up to Asheville was through some pretty nice country. Maybe I should look around the Asheville area a bit before heading home."

"It's a comfortable place. Not too much crime. Not too much gang activity. Certainly not like Atlanta has."

A movement in the lobby caught my eye. Two uniformed cops were taking someone out in handcuffs. When Detective Franks spotted them, he rose and went out to see what was going on, returning a few short minutes later with the news that a guest had been busted while smoking pot in his room. The pungent smell had attracted a maid's attention and she reported it to her supervisor. He, in turn, had told the manager, and the manager had called the cops. As it turned out, there'd been suspicion for a while that a hotel employee was selling pot to the guests. This might be their big chance to discover who it was.

Our dreadlocked waitress returned and took our orders. I opted for a three layer club sandwich, french fries, and a glass of unsweet tea.

"There's sweetener on the table, hon," the waitress said.

If I'd wanted it sweet, I would've ordered sweet tea in the first place, I thought, but I kept the comment to myself. No sense starting trouble unnecessarily.

Franks ordered a truly Southern cholesterol-rich heart stopper of a cheeseburger with double bacon, home-fried 'taters, and of course, black coffee, the working cop's life-sustaining fluid. We sat back to wait for our food. The waitress's miniscule skirt spread out in a graceful arc as she whirled and headed for the kitchen. I could see she wasn't carrying a concealed weapon of any sort.

Across the café I saw the young man with the green, gold and red Rasta hat from breakfast. He was bussing dirty dishes from a table onto a large aluminum tray.

"There's that guy again." I nodded in his direction.

Franks swiveled around in his chair to take a look. "Yep, same guy that we saw at breakfast. I'll bet he works here." He was stating the obvious, maybe so I wouldn't go off and do something stupid like confront the guy.

"Don't make fun. I'm telling you that he looks familiar."

"Yeah, all those dreadlock guys look alike, don't they?" He turned back to study his menu.

"I'm going over to talk to him," I said rising from my seat.

"Don't go starting anything," Franks warned as he turned around to watch.

I threaded my way amongst the tables of lunch customers. The closer I got, the more certain I was that this was the same guy I'd met last night in Chicken Alley. And then I spotted his Day-Glo emerald green shoelaces.

As I came up next to him I said, "Hey, I want to talk to you."

The Rasta man took one look at me, and with his eyes bulging in surprise, flung the 3-foot wide tray full of dirty dishes at me with a huge crash that tumbled me to the floor amidst broken crockery and slimy leftovers. He ran from the room, almost falling as he slipped on the lobby tiles.

I was up again as fast as I could be, dripping coffee, pudding, and food scraps, chasing after the guy who I now knew was our assailant. Why else would he run?

I skidded around the corner into the lobby and saw the Rasta rat dive left into a skinny alcove. Behind me, I heard Franks, "Hold up, Bones! This guy's mine!"

Too late. I was determined not to lose the guy. I entered the alcove and found a narrow staircase leading down in several corkscrew turns that obscured the bottom. There was no other way for him to have gone, so I followed as fast as my footing would allow.

The stairs were wet and slippery, and there was no hand rail. This route wasn't supposed to be taken at high speed. I skittered to a stop at the bottom. Light was dimmer here, but I was in a tunnel hallway that ran the length of the building. At intervals along it were the hotel's internal service areas: prep kitchens, an industrial laundry facility, the liquor lock-up. At the far end of the tunnel was the loading dock, its double doors spread wide to the daylight. My guy was doing his utmost, running toward that open air and escape. I pounded down the hallway after him, yelling. "Hey, you! Stop!"

Behind me, someone tumbled down the stairs with a roar of creative cursing. Franks. I kept going. He was on his own.

The running Rasta grabbed a steel rack of serving trays and kitchenware that stood to one side, jerked it from the wall, and dropped it directly into my path. It hit the ground with a crash. Equipment flew in all directions.

My speed wouldn't allow me to stop. I didn't hesitate, but tried to leap over it. Unfortunately, I wasn't going quite fast enough. My foot caught on something and down I went. More crashing. Another tumble and I rolled to my feet shaking free of the debris. The Rasta was at the tunnel's end by then. He shot out the door, took a turn, and disappeared from view.

I arrived a second later. There was no one in sight. I stood alone on an empty loading dock that was flanked by a couple of huge green dumpsters.

Franks arrived with gun in hand, panting and as red in the face as a black man could be. "Where'd he go?"

"He's gone," I gasped out. "He got away. See, I told you it was him."

"All right, all right." Pant, pant. "You made your point."

I rubbed it in. "He wouldn't have run if he wasn't the guy."

"That's enough." Pant, pant. "I said you made your point. I'm going back to talk to the hotel manager. Find out who that guy is. We'll pick him up before the day is out. Asheville's not all that big."

Franks tucked his little hand gun back into an ankle holster, pulled his pants leg down around it, and walked slowly back the way we had come, still trying to catch his breathe. He seemed to have developed a bit of a limp.

"You know," he wheezed, "I'm beginning to think you're a victim like you said, not the perp after all."

Well, that was something. There being nothing else for us to do down in the tunnel, we made our way back up the winding stairs. I followed along, seriously disappointed. Besides, I wanted to finish my action-packed Asheville Pisgah Hotel lunch.

Chapter 11 – The Bradfords

Back up in my sixth floor room, with the permanently sealed windows that kept despondent guests from taking that hopefully fatal but perhaps only crippling dive, I had time by myself to consider all that had happened.

In coming to Asheville, I had been looking forward to a quiet and relaxing weekend hanging out with other genealogists, catching up on professional gossip, and perhaps even learning some new techniques.

It had turned into anything but that. Why do all my innocent excursions turn into life threatening adventures? What was it about me that attracted other people's issues and traumas into my orbit? Was my karmic account that much in arrears?

Lunch had certainly been eventful. After a while, I had gotten my adrenalin back under control and finished the club sandwich as planned, but my mind continued racing. Who was that guy? What game was afoot, to paraphrase the great Sherlock? What had started us into that crazy chaser-chasee relationship? Had last night's events been a simple, random criminal act, or was there a subtext involved which I didn't yet know about? If so, what could it be?

Did I have something he wanted? Doubtful. My laptop had been in my hotel room and the only thing he could have gotten last night was a very little bit of cash and a couple of credit cards. I'm pretty easy going, not much of a fighter. All he had to do was ask politely and I'd have probably handed it over. That length of pipe was overkill. Did I really say that?

My wallet? That was what he demanded, but then he'd left without it. That was weird. Yes, he'd called for it, but he had me too addled right off by beating on my cranium with his piece of pipe. How could I respond logically with my brain so freshly scrambled?

And there was the question of whether he had been working on his own as a freelancer, or if he'd been set in motion by someone else with a nefarious plan. No, that was altogether too paranoid a thought stream, even for me. I wasn't going down that road. There was no evidence pointing in that direction. Besides, these were all questions for Detective Franks to answer. I wasn't qualified.

After a quick shower, I decided to buckle down to my self-assigned task of researching North Carolina bastardy bonds. More specifically, I wanted to see what lurked in the post-bellum history of Buck Bradford's randy errant forebear. It promised to be an interesting hunt.

Booting my laptop computer, I easily got onto the hotel's free wireless network. I started playing the Elmore James album I'd downloaded the other day, and with his raw electric slide guitar blues in my ear, I did a quick general search for Buncombe County court records, and was directed to a list of relevant sites. Expanding my search by adding the words "bastardy bond," I hit the magical return key. The results list immediately focused in surprising and highly satisfying ways.

One of the first sites to show up was a birth records page entitled *Appalachian American Genealogy.* It listed information from Georgia, North Carolina, South Carolina, and Tennessee.

Jumping down to the North Carolina section, I found instructions on how to order a birth certificate from Vital Records in Raleigh, a table that listed counties which had databases searchable through Ancestry.com, and which counties had scanned or transcribed records of apprenticeship, bastardy bonds, and delayed births. Pay dirt! The bastardy bonds listing for Buncombe County spanned the years 1824 through 1879. This was turning out to be a much easier investigation than I'd anticipated.

Less than half an hour later, I had found listings for a bastardy case involving Dixon Alton Bradford as the named father. From there, I was able to link to digital image files of the original documents. The mother of the illegitimate child was one Emma Lester, and every place her name appeared in an image shot of a relevant document, it was followed by "(col)." I assumed that meant she was African-American, which I hadn't expected. The year was 1871. Considering the times, only a few years after the Civil War and the emancipation mandated by President Lincoln, there had to be some serious black/white issues here, too. At that point in my research and without any specific evidence, I would have to bet she'd been born a slave.

From what Buck had said, much of the bastardy bond material still hadn't been digitized and put online for easy retrieval. Nonetheless, I was able to find images of pertinent documents with one or both names on them. They were stored as jpg and gif graphic files. I captured all the relevant images to my hard disk and continued searching. My goal was to progress forward in time from the earliest documents to the present. It looked like I was going to have some intriguing news about his errant forebears for Buck.

After an hour or so poking around on the Internet that afternoon, I'd managed to drift off into several other interesting but irrelevant topics. That's how my ADHD works. I learn lots about a great many things, but in a somewhat disjointed way. When my eyes finally began to cross, I decided to quit and take a nap. I shut everything down, then decided I wasn't too tired after all. Maybe I was just hungry.

I went back downstairs to the conference rooms to see what my colleagues were up to. Perhaps I could organize a dinner outing to one of Asheville's many excellent restaurants, hopefully without a serving of mayhem as a side dish.

Chapter 12 – Scene of the Crime

When the afternoon sessions were over, several of us decided to go downtown for dinner together. It wasn't that the hotel's cafe wasn't any good. It's that we were visiting a town famous for its restaurants and varied cuisines, and the better idea was to go sample some of it.

Our dinner group consisted of myself, Vivian and Buck Bradford, the bright and personable amateur genealogista Marcie Morrisette, Theron Quince, and Fanny Quinlan-Bolt, the conference's Internet expert. We were enough for three couples, only one of which, the Bradfords, was formally paired.

We began with an inquiry at the front desk. The desk clerk, a tall, cadaverous young fellow, was very helpful. Although he himself looked like he never ate at all and existed solely on the clean mountain air, he knew quite a bit about the local restaurants, their varied cuisines, and their typical price ranges.

"What kind of food are you folks looking for anyway?" he asked in a pleasant North Carolina twang.

Not knowing the local scene, our responses were kind of vague. We ended up with several recommendations, deciding in the end for Indian food at a place called Mela on Lexington Avenue, a few short blocks from the hotel.

***

My dinner companions were a varied bunch.

Marcie Morrisette showed up at various genealogical events in Georgia, Alabama, North and South Carolina. She was an enthusiastic and not unskilled amateur researcher, and many of us thought we'd soon welcome her into our professional ranks. I certainly hoped so, since I found her stimulating and that would throw us together more often. And of course, I was a man, too, however much emotionally battered, and somewhere deep down in my psyche I wanted to start dating again. She could turn out to be a comfortable casual companion to be seen at intervals. Another of my bachelor fantasies.

Theron was a dry academic type. He came complete with carved meerschaum pipe and a tweed jacket with leather elbow patches. I didn't know anything about his home life, if he were married, divorced, gay, or something else as yet unknown and unnamed. What I did know was that he was highly respected for his erudition and that he appeared on many a conference's speaker program. I also knew that he wasn't invited to lecture because he was entertaining. He wasn't, as I'd seen for myself in his lecture earlier today.

As far as Fanny Quinlan-Bolt was concerned, she was an unknown quantity for me. I'd never met her before, but I'd heard her name dropped by several people citing her as their Internet research maven. Buck had her lined up to speak tomorrow afternoon on the Internet and the quickly growing number of genealogical websites, so she had to know something. I was planning to attend her lecture.

Fanny wasn't flashy, wasn't dumpy, wasn't tall, or short, beautiful, or ugly. She was a motherly-looking type of woman, someone who, upon first meeting, you'd be perfectly comfortable putting your faith in, believing anything she said, and accepting a homemade oatmeal cookie from. She claimed to be "just a country girl," and perhaps it was her isolated rural lifestyle that had encouraged her to go online and learn all she could about researching from an isolated location.

"Where'd we lose Nadia?" Marcie asked conversationally as we strolled away from the hotel.

The question surprised me. Why would anyone want to see a murder crime scene? Not my favorite hangout, for sure. Besides, I'd already been there.

"I could show you, I guess, but . . . is that really something you want to do? Don't you think that request is a bit morbid?" I asked her. "We're supposed to be out having a good time."

"I was curious, that's all." Marcie turned to the others enthusiastically. "What do you folks say?"

Theron seemed neutral, but "terminally uninterested" might have been a better description. Fanny was intrigued, perhaps because of her lack of real world stimulation. And Vivian? Her eyes bugged out and she had a look of terror on her normally bland face.

"That's three out of five," tallied Marcie. "Let's go. Why not?"

"But, Buck . . ." Vivian tried to assert herself.

"Come on, Viv." Buck did his best to reassure her. "I'll hold your hand." He reached for her hand but she snatched it back, folded her arms momentarily, then reluctantly placed her hand in his. They continued walking along side by side, but not close to one another as she tried half-heartedly to hold him back in a minor battle of wills.

I thought Marcie's request was a bit weird to start with, but it seemed to be what my dinner companions wanted. I turned toward Chicken Alley, scene of the recent unpleasantness.

When was it that Nadia was killed? It seemed like a long time ago, but I knew that it hadn't even been 24 hours since. A lot had happened between then and now. Breakfast with Detective Franks, my lecture, a chase through the hotel's innards, the loss of our prime suspect, the afternoon's research on bastardy bonds. And now I was headed back to relive the event with a gang of curious after-the-fact rubberneckers.

The sky began a subtle color change into lighter pastels as we headed down Broadway. The night wasn't far away. Neither was Chicken Alley, and I found myself feeling a bit edgy as we approached it.

My earlier questions came up again, almost obsessively. Why had Nadia been murdered? What was the point? Or was there no point to it at all? Had it been a random act of violence like the drive-by that took my pregnant wife from me? Was it really your basic street robbery that went wrong?

And what about that Rasta guy back at the hotel? He obviously had a legit job. Did he really need the meager amount of extra cash he would've gotten from me?

Yes, I was out in the world on a junket, but it wasn't like the old days when we carried a thick wad of cash and traveler's checks with us. I'd brought a few bucks in cash along for incidentals, but primarily, I had credit cards for my trip. That guy had been risking a lot for potentially very little, but I guess that's part of the street robbery game. He was playing the odds and hoping for the best.

I never understood crime as a calling, a vocation, or even as an entertainment or hobby. An entertainment? Well, maybe if a person was addicted to adrenalin as their drug of choice. Maybe the perp was physically addicted to a demanding mistress like heroin or meth. And there was always the case to consider of Jean Valjean from Alexander Dumas' *Les Misérables* who stole a loaf of bread for his starving children. But that was probably a rarity these days. Besides, the guy had a job at the hotel and probably got free meals.

Now if you're talking about the theft of millions, the rip-off of a mega-corporation or a nation, the grand political bribe, the aluminum briefcase full of drug money, that's a different story altogether. It might be worth the risk to set yourself up in splendor for the rest of your life. I remembered the old saying, "You might as well be hung for a sheep as a lamb."

But street crime? Petty crimes like breaking and entering, stealing a school kid's lunch money? There simply isn't enough profit potential to balance against the risk of capture, prosecution, and incarceration, perhaps even death if the perp happened to pick on a victim with a pistol in his pocket. There were thousands of concealed carry permits issued to law-abiding citizens in North Carolina every year.

In the early twilight, Chicken Alley was partially shadowed by the old brick buildings that the alley ran between. It wasn't a sinister venue yet, but I could feel it would become so when the sun set completely.

Vivian had tucked in closer to her husband, and now gripped his hand in both of hers. She seemed inordinately disturbed, though there didn't seem to be any particular reason. Maybe she was psychically sensitive.

Local legend had it that the alley was haunted by the ghost of one Dr. Jamie Smith who was killed in a bar-room confrontation in 1902. Not being superstitious, I didn't put much stock in ghost stories myself, but I recognize that some people take that sort of thing very seriously. Besides, it was a good tourist draw for Asheville.

As we approached the yellow crime scene tape strung around the exact spot of last night's attack, I saw a dark stain on the pavement. Nadia's blood? What else could it be? It shook me a bit, but because of the stark reality of what happened here, not because of lurking spirits. I looked up and down the alley to see if our mugger had decided to join us. There was no one but the six of us. There being security in numbers, we were probably safe from further random attack. At least I hoped so.

"Here we are," I told my companions. "This is the exact spot." I pointed to the dark stain. "That's . . ." I didn't get a chance to finish. Vivian cut me off.

"Don't say it. I don't want to hear it!" she wailed, dragging at her husband. "Let's get out of here." Poor Buck.

Not at all reluctantly, I turned toward the near end of the alley where it spilled out onto Woodfin Street. The others followed, Vivian swinging around me and taking the lead with Buck in tow.

***

The twilight waned, the sun set, and Asheville's denizens came out in force. As Detective Franks had said, there were dreadlocks to be seen everywhere. Long dreads, short dread, dreads on blacks and whites alike, dreads on young women as well as young men, dreads on oldsters, too. Only occasionally did a person look like a "real" Rasta, whatever that looks like. In Asheville's hip community, dreadlocks were a fashion statement, not a spiritual commitment.

We made our way up Broadway's cobbled sidewalk to Mela's huge, ornately-carved wooden door with a sign that announced "Authentic Indian Cuisine." Once there, we were told the wait for a table for six would be 20 minutes or so, and that if we left to walk around, we'd lose our place in line. I was hungry and told my companions we should try another place, but they were set on Indian food. The group decided to wait.

Buck turned to his wife. "Vivian, did you try to get us a reservation? Anywhere?"

"I tried, honest, but they don't seem to do that in Asheville," she whined, working her shoulders around in little circles.

"Maybe you didn't try hard enough. Or didn't call the right restaurants," Buck retorted hotly.

"I must've called ten different places and none of them took reservations. One place, The Admiral, said they were booking reservations and could set us up for a weekday next month. We'd have had to drive across the river to West Asheville anyway."

So we waited.

Chapter 13 – Dinner Discussion

Dinner was great. Mela turned out to be an exceptional Indian restaurant, with delicately flavored foods and an attentive wait staff of attractive young women all draped in black. The bartendress and one waitress wore their hair in dreadlocks, the signature Ashevillian fashion statement, so it seemed.

Our discussion during dinner was wide ranging. We talked of everything from local weather patterns and the history of the Vanderbilts and Biltmore House to my genealogical discoveries of the afternoon. Buck, of course, was interested in my research into his family.

It seemed strange that a respected professional genealogist like Buck Bradford hadn't dug deeply into his own family's history. Most of us begin that way, and it's only after learning the basics by digging through our own ancestors that we branch out to other families and solving genealogical conundrums for other people.

I couldn't figure out why Buck hadn't looked into the case of Dixon Alton Bradford. Perhaps it was a simple case of denial in his family. How could a Bradford have done something so heinous as to father a child out of wedlock, "on the wrong side of the blanket" as they sometimes say? And with a former slave? Impossible. It simply wouldn't have happened. It couldn't have happened.

But it had. The proof was in the recorded case documents, jpg and gif images that were available on line for any curious and computer savvy researcher to find and capture to their own computers.

So I got to ramble on a bit about Dixon Alton Bradford and the bastardy bond case that tainted the Bradford family history back in the late 1800s. Buck looked more and more distressed as I went on. Was his sense of personal dignity being tattered? On the other hand, Vivian seemed totally uninterested, continually turning the table discussion to local architecture, the conference, even to recent news of doings in The Middle East.

I finally concluded. "And that's what I found, Buck. I'll show you the document images tomorrow. They're all on my laptop."

Buck was thoughtful. "Yes, I'd like to take a look. It's a bit embarrassing, actually, me not having done this research myself," he admitted.

Theron, our bastardy bond expert, was beside himself with glee. This was totally out of character for him. "I'm so pleased that my topic this morning was of help, Ben. I spent a great deal of time and effort developing my knowledge and skills in this area. Sometimes I felt that it was of only the barest academic interest. It's good to see my information used by a professional like yourself." Theron turned to Buck. "What have you got to say about it, Buck?"

Buck's eyebrows rose at being confronted. "Well," he stammered. "I don't know what I should say. Certainly Ben has done some good work based on your information. I didn't commission the work and hope he isn't expecting to invoice me for his time and effort." He looked my way, a concerned look on his face.

I laughed. "No, not at all. I was intrigued by the taste of the story you'd provided and had a great time poking around online. I learned a lot. You can have copies of everything I found. After all, it's your family history, not mine." I thought for a second, then added, "Of course, if you want to buy my dinner…" He didn't.

After dinner and a final round of drinks, we paid our individual tabs, and with receipts in hand for tax deduction purposes, headed out into the cooler evening air and back to the conference hotel. Though many conferences produce little of value except camaraderie and vague drunken memories for me, I felt like I'd accomplished something during the day instead of wasting time as usual.

Ben Bones & the Conventional Murders

Day 3 – Saturday

Chapter 14 – The Lesters

I awoke early the following morning feeling refreshed and clear. I'd had a single beer with dinner and there was no agonizing and dulling hangover. Could this be a sign? A new way of life for me? It was something to think about, maybe even work on. But for now, back to work.

To keep track of who the people were and their relationships one to another, I opened my genealogy software and created a family tree for Emma Lester and her descendants. It helps me to be able to see things spread out visually as facts and generations emerge from the historical mists.

Once online, I began my search for Emma in the 1860 Slave Schedule for North Carolina. Nothing there, as I'd expected. Even if she had been alive at the time, she wouldn't have been listed by name. The schedules listed the name of the slave owner, but the slaves were only identified by age and sex. Unless I knew her owner's name, that was a hopeless avenue. I didn't have a clue. On a hunch, I searched for the family name Lester in the 1860 census, hoping to find Emma's master. Again, I found nothing. The Lester name was perhaps one she made up or took for herself after Emancipation.

Hoping that record keeping had improved after the Civil War, I searched the 1870 census for Buncombe County, North Carolina. There she was, living independently on Pine Street in Asheville.

When I went to the 1880 census, there she was again, 10 years older and still living in Asheville. And with a 9 year old son named Lincoln Bradford Lester. I added him to my genealogy program, along with a cite for the source of my information. That had been too easy. It had to get tougher. And that's exactly what it did as I continued to trace the illegitimate line forward through time from Emma's first appearance.

According to the census, Emma Lester was working as a cook in 1880. Although illiterate, she had found a way to provide for herself and her son. She was a survivor.

There was more data for me in this census too, because the government also asked for the birthplace of the mother and father of each person listed. Though their names were still a mystery, I now knew that both her parents had been born in North Carolina. That was something, and better than nothing at all.

The trail became trickier in 1890. Unfortunately for genealogists, the 1890 census data was unavailable. There'd been a fire in the basement of the Commerce Building in Washington, D.C. in 1921, and much of the unprotected 1890 census records had been destroyed, first by the fire, and then by the water used to quench the flames. In the period spanning from 1932 to 1935, the remainder of the 1890 census records were conscientiously destroyed by civil servants thinking they were doing their proper duty for the citizenry by cleaning the debris out. They were not, but by the time the succession of official gaffes was noted, it was too late. The records were gone. A national genealogical treasure had been lost.

But a determined genealogist is not fazed by gaps in the record. We leap those troublesome gaps in a single bound, or at least try to. It might take several hops to get across, but I'd find a way. As the Buddhist GPS unit in my car says with total equanimity when I miss a turn, "Recalculating," and a new route to the goal is searched out, found, and followed. This was a small gap, and not insurmountable. I steadied myself for the jump, took a deep breath, and leaped via a click of my computer's mouse, directly to the census for 1900.

Emma was 47 when I caught up with her in 1900, still working as a cook, and seemingly the head of a household. Two people were living with her at the Pine Street address: a son named Lincoln Bradford Lester, identified as a 29-year old baker, and Olivia Bennefield, a 26-year old Mulatto daughter-in-law whose occupation was listed as housekeeper. Both Lincoln and Olivia were literate.

Another fact of interest was that in the intervening 20 years since the 1880 census, Emma had learned to read and write.

By 1910, Emma had disappeared from the census record. The Lesters were still at the same address though, so I have to assume Emma acquired the house during her lifetime. Her son Lincoln was still in the house, along with 19 year old Willis Bradford Lester, though Olivia Bennefield was not. Perhaps she had died of some disease or in childbirth, which was not uncommon in those days of primitive medical practice. That particular fact was not of census concern however. They only wanted a count of the living.

Things became more interesting in the 1920 census. Willis, by then 29 years old and a cabinetmaker with his own business, had married a woman named Catherine Finnegan, who was 20 years old. She had been born in Belfast, Ireland and was of course white. Her occupation was listed as housekeeper. She could read and write.

The saga continued into the 1930s. Lincoln B. Lester was gone by then. Willis was 39 years old, now the head of the family, still married to Catherine, and the father of a son and three daughters. One of the daughters, Elizabeth, had married a Scotsman, David McIntyre, who was listed as a son-in-law.

Interestingly, all the children in that illegitimate line from Emma Lester had been given the middle name of Bradford. I had no doubt that it was a stab at the white Dixon Alton Bradford and his family for creating the line so irresponsibly in the first place. The Lesters refused to forget. The Bradford name rang loud and clear down through the years and subsequent generations.

But that was enough for now. I'd wrung out all the census information, or so I thought. I shut my laptop off and headed downstairs to the hotel café for a late breakfast.

Chapter 15 – Breakfast Revelations

A bountiful southern breakfast lay before me: scrambled eggs, home fries, bacon, sausage biscuit with gravy. My early morning research had given me an appetite.

As I started to dig in, Detective Franks materialized and took a seat in the chair across from me.

"Howdy," he said jauntily. "How's my main 'person of interest' doing this morning?"

Almost gagging, I gulped down my mouthful of eggs without chewing.

"You're kidding, right? I'm still on your short list?"

"Not really. Just jerking your chain a bit," he said with a smirk as he leaned back in his chair. I hoped one of its legs would break off, but I kept the thought to myself.

"Well, cut it out, will you? It's not funny. A friend of mine got killed and I'm in the middle of all the confusion. It's hot enough in the frying pan without you adding more boiling oil to the mix."

He waved a hand in the air to attract a watron's attention. After ordering a breakfast like mine, only the "man-sized" version, he came out with some investigative news.

"I went and spoke with the manager yesterday. Had some long Latin name." He consulted a little spring-bound notebook he pulled from his pocket. "Marco de Luna y Garcia-Lopez. Nice fella. Very helpful. He was appalled that one of his boys might be involved in all this. Said he'd get with his Human Resources people and identify that Rasta guy for me. I should have full info on him a little later today. I wish all my cases could be solved that simply."

"Great. So who was it? No one I'd know, right? And don't you need a warrant to get that information?"

"A warrant? Yes, sometimes. But we get a lot of local cooperation, particularly at places with lots of volume traffic that make for popular crime venues," Franks explained. "This guy is a local kid. Lived here all his life and this was his first real job. Been working at the hotel about two years with no problems at all. Marco called him 'a steady, hard-working self-starter.' They thought pretty highly of him, though their attitude has changed a bit due to recent events. They also thought he might have had a hand in some dope sales, but no one's reported anything specific as yet."

"Interesting," I said, though not really interested. I just wanted the fellow caught and charged with Nadia's murder. That would begin to satisfy me.

"So what have you been up to?" He was full of questions, this detective, but that was his job, wasn't it? He had to know everything that was going on in the neighborhood, probably in all of Asheville and maybe even out in the surrounding county. The more he knew beforehand, the less he'd have to dig up later. But I did have news for him.

"I dug around in the online Buncombe County records yesterday and found some fascinating stuff. Do you know anything about bastardy bonds?"

Franks shook his head.

"Well, that's how they used to do things when a kid was born out of wedlock… 'on the wrong side of the blanket,' as they used to say."

"Yeah," Franks said thoughtfully. "I heard that expression a long time ago. My mother used it, but I never knew 'xactly what it meant."

"Anyway, the county didn't want the expense of raising the kid, so they made some serious effort to find the father and hold him responsible. As it turns out, Buck Bradford, our illustrious leader, had a rogue of an ancestor, one Dixon Alton Bradford, who was named in a bastardy case soon after the Civil War. In 1871, in fact. The woman involved was an emancipated slave named Emma Lester. The online archive was pretty amazing and I was able to capture digital image scans of all the relevant court documents. Cool stuff."

I was on a roll, so I kept going. "And get this: the Lester family used the name 'Bradford' as the family's standard middle name ever since. They all have it. Made them easy enough to track down through time. I suspect it was an insulting slap at the Bradford clan, a grudge they've held right down the line."

Franks continued to shovel his breakfast in while I rattled on, nodding his head and grunting occasionally to show he was actually paying attention. He waved his hand at the waitress for more coffee.

"Unfortunately, the trail ran out with the 1930 census, the last one to be released to the public. There's some more digging to do. I plan to hit it again later this afternoon."

A tall, beanpole of a man with straight shoulder length black hair and a pencil line mustache threaded his way to our table.

Franks set his fork down on what was left of his breakfast and shook the man's hand as he introduced us. The man wore bright yellow pants, a black jacket, a brilliantly white fancy dress shirt and a bolo tie snugged up tight to his neck with a huge chunk of malachite set in a silver slide. A matching malachite ring adorned the long middle finger of his right hand.

"This here's Marco, the hotel manager I was telling you about. How're they hangin', Marco? Que pasa?"

Marco snorted derisively, adding in a sing-song South or Central American lilt, "Detective, you know better than to ask me such a question." He winked at me while asking Franks, "Who is your handsome young friend?"

I had the feeling I was merely a sex object, what with the wink and the comment.

Franks handled the situation for me. "This here be Ben Bones. He's a famous gen'ologist." He laughed. "And he solves crimes for a hobby, looks like."

The man made a slight bow in my direction, then turned his full attention to Franks.

"My people say that the fellow you're interested in, this Oliver Cobb, called in sick this morning. Said he'd be in this afternoon. We've a computer problem in the HR office, but I should have his personnel information for you after a while.

Are you attending the conference? If so, it shouldn't be hard to find you."

"Yeah, I'll be sticking around for a while. At least until I get that info from you. I appreciate the help, Marco."

"It's only fair for me to help you out once in a while. You've been good to us at times," Marco said with a shrug. "You know, we've thought for a while that the boy might be involved in selling drugs to some of our guests, but no one has seen anything," and after a pause he added, "…if you know what I mean. No one ever knows anything about anything. Nada. Did you perhaps learn something from the arrest yesterday?"

Franks nodded affirmatively. "Oh, yeah. The guy said he'd bought the weed off'n some young dude in a Rasta hat. I think we got probable cause now to search Cobb's locker and all such as that. This is a respected Asheville hotel, but once in a while we hear rumors about guests and dope. This is the first solid lead we've been able to get here though."

Marco stood up straight and looked around the café. Spotting something wrong somewhere, he said, "I've got to take care of a problem. I'll find you later." And he was gone, off to hassle some minimum wage worker about an insignificance which he no doubt thought was important for the survival of the hotel's impeccable reputation.

Chapter 16 – A Tangled Web

Scanning the conference program, I saw that the next lecture I planned to attend, on military pensions, was starting in a few minutes. I had a research job coming up in Virginia that involved finding and claiming a Confederate soldier's Civil War pension. I didn't know how to go about it yet, though I figured I'd be an expert by the time the job was done.

I headed for Vance-A where Colonel J. Willoughby, Retired, would hold forth. Buck Bradford, clutching a stack of manila file folders to his chest, stopped me on the way.

"Hey, Ben, got a minute?"

"Sure. What's up? I'm on my way to hear Willoughby."

"Oh, that guy." Buck rolled his eyes. "What I wanted to tell you is that the conference committee is putting a CD together. Y'know, compiling all the lectures into a reference work that people can buy from the society. Can we use the tape from your session yesterday?"

That caught me off guard. "I didn't know I was being recorded."

"We've been recording everyone. Didn't you read your contract?"

"Well," I said sheepishly. "I sorta skimmed over it."

Buck laughed. "I'd expected more attention to details from you. Got to be careful what you sign these days. I don't know the exact quote, but do you remember the Woody Guthrie line about being robbed with a gun or a fountain pen? Not that I was trying to rob you."

"Yeah, you're right," I abashedly agreed. "So you want to use my stuff? It wasn't near as substantive as some of the other sessions."

"We'd like to use it. You're well known enough that your name would add to the credibility of the CD. What do you say?"

I laughed. "Flattery will get you everywhere, Buck. Sure, go ahead and use it."

In lawyerly fashion, Buck opened the top folder and whipped out a sheet of paper. "I've got an additional release for you to sign. Got a pen?"

I looked it over and asked, "If I've already signed the presenter contract with the recording clause, why do you need this, too?"

"It's something the society's lawyer recommended. Just for clarity."

"And I'm not getting anything extra for my permission, right? To be honest, I could use the increase."

Buck shook his head. "I can give you a couple of copies of the completed CD. The profit is gonna go to our local group, not to individuals."

I signed, and with that formality taken care of, Buck eased up a bit.

"I wanted to ask you something," I said. "I've been digging into that Dixon Alton Bradford character, the guy who caused that embarrassment for your family just after the Civil War. The woman involved was a former slave named Emma Lester, and all her descendants carried the Bradford name as their middle names ever since. You know anything about that?"

Buck's forehead wrinkled and he stood in the hall looking thoughtful for a few seconds. "That's odd. Bradford was my wife's middle name, before we were married. Vivian Bradford McIntyre. She could well be related to that Emma Lester. A distant descendant. Stranger things have been discovered through genealogy."

"So now she's Vivian Bradford McIntyre Bradford?" That was hard to believe. I almost laughed out loud but somehow held it back.

He nodded. "Well… she goes by Vivian M. Bradford. That's what she uses on legal documents anyways. But I'm gonna have to ask her about that Bradford business. That's real interesting. It's sometimes amazing how little we know about our spouses. And me a genealogist, too. Thanks, Bones."

"Hey, no problem. I've been having a lot of fun with this stuff. Learned a great deal from Theron's lecture yesterday and using the knowledge right away has permanently added it to my bag of genealogical tricks."

"I'm glad someone is profiting from this conference, at least knowledge-wise. I think the society will be in the red when it's all over. I won't try it again without a guarantor in the wings."

"That's a good one. Where are you gonna find a rich genealogist angel?" I asked. We both laughed at that fantasy.

"Y'know, come to think of it," Buck went on, "her sister's middle name was Bradford, too. I never thought about it before. She died a couple of years ago. Some rare blood disease. Yeah... Glenda Bradford McIntyre." He paused and thought for a few seconds. "Married a guy name of Wendell Cobb from Waynesville. I think he's still around, but we're not in touch. He was just a brother-in-law I didn't have anything in common with. You know how it goes. He was an outdoors type. Did a lot of hunting and fishing. It wasn't my thing."

We stood quietly in the hall for a minute, other conference attendees threading their way around us on their way to their next sessions. Buck checked his watch and said, "You'd better get to Willoughby's lecture if you're going. It's already started. I gotta find a few more people to get releases from." He turned and headed off. I headed for Vance-A to learn about military pensions so I wouldn't look like an idiot when I started my next research assignment in a few weeks.

Ben Bones & the Conventional Murders

Chapter 17 – The Web Tightens

As it turned out, I could have learned almost everything I needed to know about military pensions on my own without listening to The Colonel, Retired, drone on for his allotted hour and a half. I'm an autodidact. Been so all my life, and as such, I could teach myself virtually anything I needed to know.

The search for someone's military pension involved the usual tedium of filling out and mailing in involved government forms and waiting for the high school graduates at the other end to read, file, and respond to them. What I learned from The Colonel were a few miscellaneous facts about where the pension records were housed. Federal pension records for the Civil War era are available from the National Archives, and there are indices online that will lead you to the right record. They would be easy enough to find.

Confederate pensions were an entirely different matter, and my upcoming Virginia pension research job would entail a more in-depth search. A Confederate veteran's pension depended on the state where the vet or his widow were living when they applied for the pension, not where he signed up to fight or the state under whose flag he fought, or even where he mustered out. Widows were allowed to apply after they had remarried as well, and they might well apply under a variety of last names. It could become real confusing real fast.

It was all interesting enough to a genealogy geek like myself, but not what I needed at the moment. Back in my room, I dropped The Colonel's lecture handout onto the pile of conference papers that was accumulating on my room's credenza and turned back to the problem at hand: the history of the Lester family after 1930. With the accompaniment of a bit of old folk blues music from Furry Lewis and Howling Wolf, of course.

I plugged my laptop in and opened the Lester genealogy chart I'd built. I'd left off with the most recently released census. At some point way back, the government head counters decided that in order to protect people's privacy, they wouldn't release complete census enumeration pages until 72 years had passed and most of those listed by name had passed on. Not a bad idea for privacy advocates, but terribly inconvenient for genealogists.

Somewhat perplexed about how to proceed from 1930 forward, I opened my browser and did a broad search for census pages. Surprise! The 1940 Census was listed along with all the others. Then I realized my error. This was the year 2012, and that meant we were exactly 72 years from the 16th census taken in 1940. The 1940 Census was out for all us genealogy geeks to peruse at our leisure.

How could I have been so dumb? I had to find it like that, by accident? I'm supposed to be a professional genealogist, and here one of the most basic of research tools had completely escaped me. Talk about "head in the sand" syndrome. I'd been so focused on everything else in my little world that I'd missed the grossly obvious. Was it creeping senility? Early Onset Alzheimer's? Too much Drambuie?

But having found it, I was going to use it, and with a vengeance. I'd find all the Asheville people I was interested in. It was merely a matter of a few mouse clicks. Maybe.

Actually, it wasn't quite that simple. The problem was that, although the census population data had been released to the public, there was no name index. The government left that daunting task to volunteer genealogical societies, and it would be years until all the indexing had been accomplished. If I wanted information, I'd have to spend however many hours were required to scan all the enumeration sheets in specific geographic areas until the relevant names revealed themselves. I ordered up a beer from room service and settled in for what I expected would be an eye-blearing search.

In the North Carolina pages, I narrowed my search criteria to the city of Asheville in Buncombe County. Luckily, in 1940, Asheville was still a relatively small town, still only a playground for the rich and a small number of the ailing who'd heard about the "invigorating mountain airs." Asheville listed relatively few enumeration sheets compared to places like San Francisco or New York City. As the red king said in Lewis Carroll's *Alice in Wonderland,* "Begin at the beginning, and go on till you come to the end: then stop." I retrieved the image for the first page and began reading.

Two beers, a club sandwich, and three tedious hours later, I still hadn't found what I was looking for. I was going cross-eyed and dreaded the idea of further line by line searching. Because of the poor government scanning, the enumerator's handwriting was sometimes too light to read, or, if dark enough, it might show as a somewhat darker scribble on a slate gray page. In many instances, the writing was simply illegible. This slogging online search was becoming a serious chore. But without a name index, it was the only way to go.

Eventually, I found the Lesters, still living in the same house on Pine Street. The house had passed down the generations. A deed search would have helped by providing details of the property transfers. Besides detailed property descriptions, there are grantor and grantee names in deeds, and sometimes even parent names. I added a deed search in the county archives to my list of additional research tasks. Something to do later if I was bored.

But things had changed in the house on Pine Street. A Lester wasn't the head of the household any longer. Instead, one David McIntyre, identified as a 35 year old white man born in Scotland, was in charge. He was married to Elizabeth Bradford Lester, who I already knew from the 1930 Census was the daughter of Willis B. Lester and Catherine Finnegan. No Willis. The picture became clearer.

Ford B. Lester, a 26 year old male Lester, still lived in the house along with his sisters Sally B. and Nigeria B., all children of Willis and Catherine. But Ford didn't control the situation.

The big surprise was that Catherine was still there, now identified as a widowed mother-in-law to David McIntyre.

It looked like I was only one generation away from the present. According to what Buck Bradford had told me earlier,

David McIntyre and Elizabeth B. had two daughters: Glenda, now deceased, and the current Vivian Bradford McIntyre Bradford. Glenda had married a Wendell Cobb from Waynesville and had died of a blood problem. Were there any children to carry on their line? Buck hadn't mentioned any kids from either marriage.

And then, a light went on in the Stygian darkness of my skull. I wasn't thinking it through clearly. It was time to resort to the most basic research tool in any genealogist's arsenal. I needed a local phone book.

I rummaged around in the credenza drawers looking for an Asheville book. Nothing. Where else might I find… Ah, yes, the bedside table. In the right-hand table, a Gideon bible. In the left, a Koran and a Buncombe County phone directory. I flipped the directory open and ran my finger down the C names. Surprise, surprise! "Cobb, Wendell" was listed in Asheville. I love it when the trail is easy to follow.

I dialed Cobb, Wendell's number.

Ring, ring, ring, ring. It rang ten times. I decided to try again later. He might be at work, or… what day was this? Saturday. Maybe he'd gone fishing. Or hadn't recovered from last night's drinking, or… anything could have happened.

Just as I was about to hang up, the ringing stopped. A raspy voice said in a thick drawl, "Cobb here. Who's that?"

"Hi. I'm Ben Bones, a genealogist at the convention in Asheville this weekend. I've been doing some research into the Lester family and I wonder if you'd answer a couple of questions."

It was quiet on the other end. I could imagine gears whirring in the man's head as he weighed the consequences of talking to a stranger about family matters.

"Lesters, eh? Yeah, I guess so. What do you want to know? I was married to a Lester girl, Glenda. She died. Damn shame. Really messed me up. Messed up my plans, if know wadda mean."

"I'm sorry to hear that. Buck Bradford told me about it."

More silence from Wendell Cobb, except for a wheeze I detected in his breathing. Cigarettes? Emphysema? And in all this clean mountain air, too.

"I was wondering if you'd had any children, you know, to carry on the Lester line."

"Yeah, we had one kid. Turned out a good-for-nothing bum. I think he's dealing dope somewhere downtown these days. We don't get along so good. I give up on him years ago. He kinda went wacky after his momma died." He snorted a laugh. "I did too, I guess, so who can blame him?"

"What's his name? Does he have a regular job anywhere?"

"Last I knew he was in some fast food joint washing dishes. He had no ambition. Quit school too soon anyway. Ollie's his name, Oliver Bradford Cobb. And don't think there wasn't a fight about that middle name neither. But it was her family tradition and all of 'em lined up against me. What could I do 'bout it? They had me by my short hairs."

"I guess that's all I needed to hear, Mr. Cobb," I said. "Thanks for your help." Oliver Cobb, I thought. Where had I heard that name before?

"Sure. It ain't nothing to me. You say you know Buck?"

"Yes. He and Vivian organized the convention I'm attending. I'll see him later today."

"Boy, that Vivian was a piece of work. She went off when he sister died, too. Never was quite the same after. It was like a part of her went with Glenda. She was ambitious though, I'll give her that. Buck now, he was more a laid back type. Nice guy, but kinda boring. Didn't know how to have a good time, if you know what I mean. But if you run into him, tell him I said hello."

"I sure will. And thanks again."

"You don't have to say nothin' to Vivian," he added.

"Yeah, sure."

He hung up.

I sat and thought about things for a bit. Glenda, Buck, Vivian, David McIntyre, Wendell Cobb, Ollie… It was an odd family group, and some of them didn't even know they were related.

Using a tool in my genealogy program, I worked out the fact that Buck Bradford and his wife Vivian were half 3rd cousins. They were related by blood through the illegitimate child and the bastardy bond legal proceedings way back in 1871. Dixon Alton Bradford, the wanton named father and progenitor of the Lester line, was Buck's 2nd great-grandfather.

Chapter 18 – Banquet Hijinks

I couldn't wait to talk to Buck. As a genealogist, he was perfectly competent to have worked all this out for himself. Any genealogist worth their salt starts out in his own lineage before taking on the rest of the world. Since he was so open and forthright about the postbellum bastardy bond, he'd probably be open about the blood relationship with his wife as well. But how could he not know? How could that be? I'd see them later at the banquet and tell them about what I'd discovered. I wondered how they'd react.

Not having any need in my life for formal attire, I hadn't brought a tux to Asheville. I didn't own one anyway. The banquet tonight wouldn't be too fancy. We were genealogists after all, and not into all the expensive trappings of wealth and power. Well, maybe a few of the more egocentric liked that sort of thing, but I wasn't one of them. In fact, I thought that Colonel Willoughby, Retired, might be the only one who wanted to "suit up" for dinner. He might show up in full regalia, all polished and fluffed up and bedecked with medals.

I took a shower, dressed in a sport shirt and slacks, combed my hair and beard and headed downstairs with my tweed sport jacket draped over one shoulder. That was as far as I ever went in looking the part. At least the jacket had leather elbow patches for that intellectual college professor look.

Downstairs, the convention crowd was milling around in the bar and spilling out into the lobby. A classical guitarist with a huge walrus mustache and a deliciously delicate touch on the fingerboard provided background music from a little platform off to one side of the room.

I spotted Buck standing near the bar with Marcie Morrisette. Well, Buck was standing anyway. We had an entire hour before dinner and Marcie already looked a bit wobbly as she clung to Buck for support. It was the final evening of the convention and she was making the most of it. Would she remember it at all tomorrow?

I started making my way through the crowd toward Buck, getting a few back slaps and hand shakes along the way. It's great being a celebrity, but it has its problems, too. An attractive woman I hadn't noticed before asked me to autograph her convention program. When I looked up from signing, she had her camera phone out and asked her equally good looking friend to snap a picture of the two of us. By the time all that was over, I saw Buck and Marcie heading out of the far end of the bar, Marcie looking extremely loose as she leaned on Buck. Oh, boy. Buck may not know how to have a good time, but Marcie could turn any event into a party. There'd be plenty of talk at breakfast tomorrow morning.

Continuing to the bar, I looked around for Vivian, I but didn't see her. I could tell her my relationship news just as well as telling Buck. They both owned the information.

"I'll have a Drambuie on the rocks," I said, against my own better judgment. Only one. I'd keep it together this evening. I could do it. I didn't want to end up on a table with a lampshade on my head, a legend in the making.

The conversation was the usual small talk and bar banter. Someone at the bar was betting he could stand an egg on its end. I wandered through the crowd continuing to look for Vivian.

Buck showed up again after a while, but only minutes before he had to get the banquet going. He was seated at the head table, and Vivian was at his side looking as frumpy as ever, and not a little angry, too. How had I missed her entrance? Maybe it was the second Drambuie.

Boring speeches, flat jokes, and rubber chicken were on the menu for the evening. I think I had another Drambuie or two. It was still dark outside when I woke up fully dressed atop the covers in my hotel room with a heavy head and a lousy taste in my mouth. I made it to the bathroom, splashed some cold water on my face, then noticed that someone had written "Good luck!" with lipstick on the vanity mirror. No signature. No phone number.

Ben Bones & the Conventional Murders

I went back to bed, this time undressing and slipping between the sheets. I'd done it to myself again.

Chapter 19 – The Other – #2

Saturday Night – After the Banquet

Downstairs in the service tunnel, the young man wearing a knit green, gold and red Rasta hat and a white hotel service jacket whipped around balancing a pile of clean plates. He approached the woman.

"Oh, Auntie. You startled me. Good to see you. Everything is going well, yes?"

"No, everything isn't going well. You really made a mess of things."

Ollie's eyebrows shot up and he furrowed his brow. "How? I did what you told me. I didn't even get the guy's wallet, y'know? He probably had a bundle."

"You know that woman is dead? Do you know that you killed her?"

Ollie set the pile of plates down on a metal rack. "Nah. Come on, Auntie. You can't be serious."

"I'm dead serious. You killed her. What were you thinking? How hard did you hit her? You were only supposed to scare her off."

"I didn't mean to. I mean..." He spread his hands in a helpless gesture. "I didn't..."

"But you did. And they know it was you. And they're looking for you."

Ollie laughed. "Yeah, that guy from last night chased me out of the café at lunch time. He chased me down through the tunnels, but I got away. That was pretty funny," he said with a broad grin.

"Not that funny. There was an Asheville homicide cop right behind him. You could've been shot."

"Nah. Come on." Ollie responded.

"I had dinner last night with the guy who chased you, the guy who was with the woman you killed Thursday night. He knows what you look like."

"I... " Ollie fumbled for words.

"Not only that, but he probably knows we're related. He's a genealogist and he can easily find out that you're my nephew. He hasn't put us together yet, but he will. He's smart. He thinks. Not like you. He puts facts together and figures things out. That's what he does for a living."

Ollie's eyes widened as he realized his aunt was telling him the dangerous truth.

"What can I do?" He backed up against the steel rack.

"You've got to go home now," she said. "Maybe go stay with friends for a few days. Maybe go to Waynesville or Charlotte. Only until the conference is over and they've all gone back where they came from."

"I can't go nowhere." He puffed out his chest. "I got my job to do. I got responsibilities now. And I'm makin' some good money on the side, too." He mimicked toking on a joint, then winked and laughed.

"Yeah, selling that weed stuff," she said in a heated stage whisper. "You want to go to jail? Get out of here and don't come back until next week."

"Calm down, Auntie. Nothing's going to happen. Everything is cool." His hands pumped in 'cool down' motion in front of him.

"You been smoking that weed yourself, too, haven't you? If you weren't so stoned, you'd know you were in trouble."

"Go away, Auntie. You're really starting to bother me. I ain't leaving." He turned his back to her, turned back to pick up his pile of plates again.

In frustration, Auntie attacked. She lunged forward and pummeled him with her fists. He hunched his back under her onslaught. Two plates fell off the pile and shattered on the concrete floor. He set the pile back down hastily on the steel rack and turned to protect himself, grabbing her by the wrists.

She writhed in his grip, furious, but he was young and strong.

"Cut it out, Auntie. Stop. Get it together." Letting go of her wrists, he shoved her backwards and away from him. "I *ain't gonna fight wit' you. You're gonna lose. I don't want to hurt you." He turned back to his plates. "Now let me work."*

Vivian looked for something, anything, to make her point more forcefully. Reaching down, she grabbed a large piece of a broken serving platter, straightened up, and took a swipe at her nephew.

Ollie felt the impact on the side of his neck. He didn't know what had hit him, didn't feel any pain. What scared him was the gusher of bright red blood that pumped from the wound: squirt, squirt, squirt. Arterial blood. Oxygen-rich blood that wasn't going to reach his brain, that wasn't going to circulate through him any longer. Blood fountained from his throat onto his plates, the rack, the concrete of walls and floor. He dropped his plates with a crash that echoed down the concrete tunnel. Clutching at his throat, he staggered and turned.

Vivian stood horrified. What had she done?

Ollie grabbed at his aunt, his blood spraying her face, her hair, her clothes, the wall behind her. He grabbed at her, his hand tangling in her hair. She wrenched herself backwards, crashing into the opposing tunnel wall, Ollie still attached to her. Blood sprayed, but the boy held on. She twisted wildly to get away. Hair tore away in his hand. Her scalp hurt.

Suddenly free, she turned and ran, ran down the tunnel toward the twin doors at the end. She hit the release bar and the door burst open. She was outside in the cool night air and away from the argument, the blood, the horror.

Day 4 – Sunday

Chapter 20 – The Ex-Rasta

I didn't sleep well Saturday night after the banquet and waking up not knowing who my mysterious guest had been. There was too much to consider, too many unsettling events in too short a time, and it had only been over the past day and a half. It all felt vaguely related, but I couldn't see the connections. That had me stuck, or perhaps unstuck, depending on how you viewed the confusion of my life.

At 3:40 A.M., I gave up on trying to sleep. All I was doing was tying myself into knots amidst the bedclothes. I figured I'd go out for an early morning walk up and down the hotel corridors and then come back to my room for a shower. That would get me downstairs to breakfast at the scheduled time. Maybe I'd drag a bit through the day, but there wasn't going to be a need for a high energy level. I might even doze off during an otherwise boring lecture. That would be a real reputation killer. Pulling on a t-shirt, jeans, and trainers without socks, I checked to be sure I had my electronic key card and phone, and headed out the door.

Going down the stairs instead of taking the elevator would finish waking me up and get my blood flowing. But with all that had happened rattling around in my head, I wasn't paying full attention en route. I missed the lobby floor and ended up down in the tunnel where the staircase came to an end. Oh, well. As long as I was here, maybe it would be a good idea to revisit the scene of my recent foot race.

The staircase I'd taken dumped me out almost midway down the tunnel's length, about half way between the loading dock's double doors and the narrow spiral service stair that descended from the lobby at the other end.

There didn't seem to be anyone around, although I could hear people in the prep kitchen. There was lots of banter and the clashing of metal utensils. I wondered if our Rasta man was in there chopping up vegetables for the hotel guests, maybe chopping up some of the guests themselves. Carefully and quietly, I went in that direction.

Reaching the opening to the prep kitchen bay, I slowly pushed the door open a bit more and stuck my head around the corner for a look.

A woman of substantial girth stood in the middle of the activity giving orders left and right. She was wrapped tightly in a white apron whose tie strings didn't quite reach around her. The gap was bridged by a piece of binder's twine. Two young men and three young women in hairnets were being kept busy chopping and wrapping cut veggies up in clear film and carrying tubs of raw vegetables to and from the walk-in cooler. There was a dreadlocked young woman, but no young Rasta man.

"What d'you want?" The supervisor had spotted me at the door. She didn't miss a thing. "If you're a guest, you're not supposed to be down here. This area is only for staff."

"Sorry. Guess I got off on the wrong floor."

"Most people have the common sense not to make that kind of mistake. Go back up to the guest floors." So irritable this early? "Why don't you get you some breakfast and stop bothering us down here. We got work to do."

She certainly had a way with people. I turned from the door, closing it gently behind me, and started down the tunnel toward the loading dock, looking into each bay as I passed.

The door next to the prep kitchen was a huge walk-in cooler. I assumed it was the back entrance to the one I'd just seen in food prep. It was oriented in a way that made that seem logical. I continued walking.

I approached the double doors to the outside world. A bulb was out and the tunnel back here was only dimly lit. There was a pungent smell in the air, like meat left out on the kitchen counter and forgotten. I stepped into something sticky, but

Ben Bones & the Conventional Murders

looking down I couldn't make out what it was. Because it was darker than the concrete of the tunnel's floor, it was easy enough to see where the stuff came from even in the dimness. It had seeped out from under the door of the next bay and spread out into the tunnel.

I inched forward toward the door, my shoes making a sucking sound as they pulled free of the goo on the floor. I gave the door a light push and it slowly swung open on well-oiled hinges. An automatic switch flicked the interior light on.

There was the young Rasta man Franks and I had chased the day before, lying on the floor in a huge puddle of reddish-brownish blood, a triangular piece of the hotel's delicately decorated ceramic dinnerware sticking out of the side of his neck. He'd bled out from a severed carotid artery. It definitely wasn't a suicide.

Standing there in the goop, a dead man at my feet, I hauled out my cell phone and dialed 911, a three digit number I had hoped I'd never have to dial again.

Chapter 21 – The Cops

I backed out of the bloody room and into the tunnel, my shoes leaving bloody footprints to show where I'd been. The smell had become more noticeable, but I suppose it was only my heightened awareness at the horror I'd discovered. Adrenalin was gushing through me, and my fight or flight thing had cranked up exponentially.

The cops arrived within minutes. Being downtown helped, I guess. If we'd been at a country bed and breakfast, they might've taken hours to arrive. But the hotel was located close to the Asheville Police headquarters.

A young officer in uniform showed up first, coming down the tunnel toward me from the lobby end with gun in hand. He'd made an official entrance. Marco, the hotel manager, followed him in a rush. They reached me and took a look into the bloody equipment bay. Marco gagged. This wasn't his usual early morning fare.

"Who are you?" the young cop asked me as he backed out of the make-shift abattoir.

"I made the 911 call. My names Bones, Ben Bones," I responded. "Wilbur Franks knows me. Can you get him over here?"

"He's on his way. Don't worry about it. He gets all these kinda calls."

At that moment, we heard a thud and a loud curse from the spiral stairway at the far end of the tunnel. Turning to look, we saw Detective Franks getting back to his feet after a tumble. He dusted himself off and headed toward us.

"Bones! What the hell are you doing up at 4 in the morning?" He looked into the equipment bay and saw the dead Rasta. He turned to face me. "You do this? Tell me the truth, now. I'll get it sooner or later." He scowled as he growled.

"No. I found him while I was exploring around the hotel. He was like that. I didn't move anything. But I made few footprints in the blood." I lifted one foot and showed him the sole of my sneaker.

"Boy, you do get into the middle of things, don't you? Now I know where all those stories of yours come from. You're a magnet for murder."

"It's not my fault," I countered. "I'm just in the wrong place at the wrong time."

"Yeah. All the time," he said.

"This is the Cobb kid?" Franks asked Marco.

"That's right. I was going to give you his personnel file this morning. Oliver Bradford Cobb. That's too bad. So young."

"He was a petty criminal. Probably had a great criminal future to look forward to. And he could've given us some answers that we desperately want. So much for solving the Nadia woman's murder easily. And now I've got this." He waved a hand at the mess.

More cops arrived along with some suits carrying hand luggage. These last were the forensics guys. They started their process. A guy who sounded like a big city Northerner who had been transplanted to the wilds of North Carolina confronted Franks.

Pointing to my footprints in the bloody goo, he asked, "Whose footprints are those?"

"They're mine," I interjected.

"Take your shoes off and give 'em to me." He opened one of his cases and pulled out a large plastic bag. "Drop 'em in here."

"What?"

The guy insisted. "You heard me. I want your shoes in this here bag."

I looked at Franks. He shrugged back at me.

A murder in Asheville required following the same protocols as a murder in New York or L.A. Step by step, clue by clue, detail by detail, the case would slowly be built piece upon painstaking piece.

The guy handed Franks a pair of blue paper booties. "And you, put these on if you wanna take a peek."

Franks did, then gingerly stepped into my footprints as he went in for a closer look.

Without touching it, he looked the body over. "Looks like he was killed with a piece of a dinner plate. You guys will have fun with that." He leaned in closer. "He's holding something in his hand. Might be a piece of towel or something. Fibers. How long do you think he's been here?"

"Whadda you think I got a crystal ball?" New York answered. "Wait a minute or two, will ya? We ain't even got started yet."

Then it hit me. I asked Marco, "Did you say the guy's name was Cobb? Bradford Cobb?"

Marco nodded, then added in his mellifluous voice with the musical Spanish accent, "Yes, but Bradford was his middle name. His first name was Oliver. Everyone here called him Ollie."

"That's the connection, Franks," I almost yelled. "Bradford! Remember I told you that that entire family maintained the middle name Bradford since the original bastardy case back in 1871?"

Franks nodded, but he didn't tie it together.

"He's one of them, too," I enthused. "He's one of the descendants down that family line. He's related to Vivian Bradford McIntyre Bradford. I'll bet he's only one or two degrees of consanguinity away from her." I paused for breath as my feeble mind began seeing the relationship clearly. "I've got it! Vivian is his aunt! Ollie Cobb is her deceased sister's son." I slapped my palm to my forehead. "I talked with his dad Wendell Cobb yesterday and didn't see it. How dumb can I be?"

Franks still didn't get it. "So what's that got to do with Nadia?"

"I don't know… yet. But it's tied in somehow. I'll betcha."

We were interrupted by the big city forensics guy. "Look at this here," he said, holding up a pair of tweezers from which hung a hank of curly brownish hair. "From the stiff's right hand. Held tight, too. If I had to guess, which I don't usually do, I'd say this was from the head of whoever killed this kid. You'd better go lookin' for a fresh bald spot on the left side of someone's head before it grows back. That person's gonna be your main suspect."

Franks nodded slowly and worked the tip of his tongue back and forth across his lower lip. He took a quick surreptitious look at the top of my head. "Yeah, that all makes some kinda sense, don't it. Okay. Thanks, Freddy. If that works out, I'll buy you a beer."

Freddy laughed. "You'll buy me dinner and a beer. I'm keeping score. You aw'ready owe me two."

Chapter 22 – My Strategy

We were finally able to put it all together: the cops, represented by veteran homicide detective Wilbur Franks; hotel manager Marco Garcia-Lopez; and yours truly, Benjamin S. Bones, vaunted Articulator of Family Skeletons and Victim/Suspect at Large.

Could Vivian Bradford somehow be involved in Nadia's murder? That sounded ridiculous. What had she to gain? Nothing that I could figure. But there was a closer relationship between Vivian and Ollie Cobb than any of us had suspected and I was sure it meant something, though I didn't know what… yet. It might come to me. Maybe not. I can be pretty insightful sometimes, but pretty dense at others. It was an interesting set of wrinkles, to be sure.

The forensic team started packing up their gear. A pair of guys in white coveralls with EMT patches had rolled a gurney in from the loading dock and were waiting for permission to take the body. The wheels of justice were beginning to grind.

Franks looked at his watch. "It's almost 6 o'clock. People should be getting up about now. I think I'll go talk to Vivian Bradford." He looked at Marco. "What room are the Bradfords staying in?"

"We comped them a room for the convention business they brought, but I don't know if they've been staying here. They live close enough to go home every night. Let's go up to the front desk and I'll get you the room number."

"Can I come along?" I asked my detective companion. I was devilishly curious to hear what the woman had to say.

Franks' face wrinkled up in an expression that told me I was nuts to even ask. "Sorry, Bones, but that's not how it works. You've been a suspect, remember? Not to say that you haven't given me a bunch of good info to work with."

But I saw a strategy. "How about this? You cuff me and drag me along to interview Vivian. Use me as a foil to jog her into saying… whatever. If she's involved in all this, she might just be surprised enough to drop her guard."

Franks rubbed his bristled chin. He hadn't had a chance to shave and looked like he'd been up all night again. He probably had been, or at least he'd been rousted out of bed far too early when this most recent murder had been reported by yours truly.

I don't know why guys bother to shave at all. Don't they realize it's a war they can never win? They might win the occasional battle for a few hours, but think of all the time, effort, and money that would be saved if all us guys went ahead and grew beards. Personally, I understood the hopelessness of the situation from the very beginning of my shaving career and gave up immediately.

Franks had a crafty look. He'd decided to go with my suggestion and reached around to grab his cuffs from the back of his belt. "That's not a bad idea. Put your hands out."

I did, and he snapped the cuffs on me.

"Not too tight?"

"No," I said thoughtfully, "but it's my first time and it feels totally weird. I'm really hampered. I can't do anything."

He laughed. "That's the idea, all right."

I didn't laugh. Standing there barefoot and in handcuffs, I felt curiously vulnerable. It was a feeling I'd never had before and I didn't like it. Where do I get these bright ideas? And why?

"Come on. Let's go see the Bradfords." He wagged a big forefinger at me. "And you keep your mouth shut. I'm the detective and I'll do the talking. Got it?"

"Yeah, I got it. But watch me. I might raise an eyebrow or two if she says something you don't catch."

He put his hammy fists on his hips. "Look'a here. I been doing this work for some 20 odd years. I don't miss nothin'," he announced with an eloquent wagging of his head.

"Yeah, sure. But this isn't like a normal murder, is it?"

"Normal? In all this time I've never seen a 'normal' murder. Every one of them is special in some way or other.

There's no such thing as a 'normal' murder. You've been watching too much television." He turned down the tunnel toward the spiral staircase. "Come on. Let's go."

Off we went, the investigator and the investigatee. That's what we were supposed to look like. But we were actually co-conspirators. Well, maybe not. He was the investigator and I was merely a stage prop. At least I wasn't a real suspect any longer… even though I was the only person who was wearing handcuffs.

Chapter 23 – Spilt Beans

The Bradfords had presumably headed to their hotel room after last night's banquet. It being 7 A.M. by then, we took a quick look into the buffet area to see if they had come down for an early breakfast. Not seeing them there, we headed for the room Marco had told us they were in. There was no sound from inside. Maybe they liked to sleep in late. Franks knocked on the door.

No response. He knocked again, a bit more insistently.

The door cracked open, chained against an unwanted invasion. Buck Bradford's sleep disfigured face peeked out. Recognizing us, he slipped the chain free and opened the door wide as he backed away. We entered and the door swung closed with a click behind us.

Buck's eyes went wide when he saw the cuffs on my wrists.

"What's going on? Bones... what?" He was startled. We were getting the right reaction but from the wrong person.

"I need to talk with Mrs. Bradford," Franks intoned in an official baritone as he flashed his badge.

Buck rubbed the sand out of the corners of both his eyes simultaneously with his index fingers. He was a balanced kind of guy. "She's not here. She said she wasn't feeling well after the banquet and went home last night. I'm not sure she'll be here today."

Franks and I exchanged glances.

"Can I ask you a few questions, Mr. Bradford?" Franks asked.

"Sure, but I've got to have a shower before going out to meet my public. It'll help me wake up."

"This will only take a few minutes," Franks said. "Did you know about Glenda Cobb's son?"

"I knew they'd had a kid, yeah. Why?"

"You didn't tell me about that," I tossed into the conversation. Franks gave me a dirty look. I shut up.

"I didn't tell you because I didn't think it was important. Is it?" Buck said.

Franks said, "It seems like it was important to someone. The kid, Ollie Cobb, was the prime suspect in Nadia Worthington-Lamond's murder on Thursday night, and this morning he was found dead himself. It wasn't a suicide."

Buck was suddenly wide awake without his shower. "You're kidding, right? Is this a joke?" He turned to me. "It's a joke, right, Bones? And what's with the handcuffs anyway?"

Franks answered before I got my big mouth in gear. "Murder isn't something I joke about, Mr. Bradford. Solving murders is what I do for a living. Oliver Bradford Cobb was found dead early this morning, and it wasn't suicide and it wasn't an accident either. Someone killed him. We need to find out who and why."

"Well, why come to me?" Buck didn't see any connection. "I was here sleeping since after the banquet. I'd had a couple of drinks and went out like a light. It had been a long day."

"But your wife wasn't here, right?" Franks asked. "Where was she?"

"She said she felt ill and went home to her own bed. We live close enough... up in Weaverville."

"I need to talk to her."

"You think she killed her own nephew? That's plain stupid." Buck was obviously appalled that Franks would even consider such an outrageous idea.

"We, er... I just need to talk with her." Franks reiterated as he gave me another eye-rolling and meaningful look.

At that instant, we heard the click of the electronic door latch being released. The door swung open and Vivian stood on the threshold. She looked like she'd been through hell. Her face was swollen unevenly in various places, particularly in the dark bags under her eyes, and the whites of her eyes themselves were like maps with myriad twisting roads laid out in red. She wore a plain tan shift, belted around her substantial middle, and tan low-heeled shoes. Her head was wrapped in a colorful scarf that imitated a turban with a tail that hung down to her neck on the left side.

"What… what's going on?" she asked in a cracked voice. "Why are these people here, Buck?"

And then she noticed my handcuffs.

"Ben! What's happened? Will someone please tell me what's going on?"

Buck moved to her side and put his arm around her. "Ollie's dead. Murdered."

Vivian eyes bugged out and she immediately burst into tears. There was no transition to it. One instant she was demanding answers and the next she was in a full bore breakdown.

Her extreme mood was unsettling. Even Franks, who had undoubtedly seen plenty of uncontrolled emotion during a 20 year investigative career was taken aback.

Buck tried to comfort her. "Honey, what's wrong? Tell me."

"It was all for you, Buck," she managed to sniffle out between sobs that convulsed her body. "I did it all for you."

Franks gave me another one of those looks. It told me that he knew we were on the verge of the truth about something, though the "something" was still hidden. My handcuff strategy might have softened her up, but it was the abrupt announcement of her nephew Ollie's murder that had flipped her emotional switch.

"It was an accident. I didn't mean to do it, but I was so upset. I only hit him once. That was all." An unearthly wail came from deep within her and the flood of tears intensified.

"What are you talking about, Viv?" Buck asked.

"You're such a dud, you know? No ambition at all. You never wanted anything but to study all those old books. The convention wasn't even your idea." She sniffled mightily. "When the Society voted for it, you had to chair it 'cause you're the President, but who set it all up, made all the arrangements, contacted all the speakers? Me, that's who.

"I hadn't expected Filgurst and his contract. He found out about our convention and came here with his own plan. But when I heard about it, I saw it as your big chance, but it was a chance you would never take. I decided to do something for you, Buck. For you! To help you get the contract and change our lives."

She reached around to grab the tail of her turban to wipe at her eyes. It came loose and she grabbed it with both hands to hold it in place atop her head.

"I hit him and he started bleeding. It was horrible. I didn't mean to do it."

Franks produced a handcuff key and made to unlock my bracelets. He turned his face toward Vivian. "Mrs. Bradford," he said, "You're under arrest for the murder of Oliver Cobb."

"NOOOOO!" she wailed. "This is all your fault, Bones. I never would've been caught if…" and she sprang at me. The agility and force in the little woman was positively amazing. She hit me like a line backer, her hands going for my throat, and we went down in a writhing pile. I twisted this way and that, but she was quick and got her hands around my neck. They were little hands, but strong, and I could feel her thumbs as they tried to crush my Adam's apple.

There was little I could do with my hands cuffed. I tried to drive them up between her arms, but with her dense, compact body on top of me, I could hardly move. I rolled to the left and to the right trying to throw her off me.

Franks sprang into action. He dropped the handcuff key, grabbed her from behind, threw his elbow around her throat in the classic cops' choke hold, and hauled her backwards. Her turban fell to the floor as the three of us scrambled around like cats in a sack.

Buck was screaming at Vivian to stop, but she was simply out-of-control wild.

It seemed like an hour, but it was probably only seconds later that she sagged to the floor exhausted. The emotional toll, coupled with the unaccustomed strenuous effort of her physical attack, simply wore her out.

Franks was on his back with her full weight on top of him, his arm still crooked around her neck in an attempt to cut off blood flow to her brain so she'd pass out. She didn't pass out, but lay there inert until he rolled her off to the side and onto the floor. She lay there gasping like a dying fish, her dress pulled up onto her heavy thighs, her turban abandoned in a heap beside her. There were no more tears.

I grabbed the handcuff key off the floor and with some Houdini-esque difficulty, managed to unlock the left cuff. The right hand side was easier after that. I handed the cuffs to Franks.

He snapped one cuff onto Vivian's right wrist first, pulled it around behind her, then gently helped her to a standing position. She looked defeated. I saw a raw bald spot on the left side of her scalp where hair had been ripped out. I pointed to it. Franks merely grunted. He pulled her other hand behind her and snapped the other cuff onto it. She stood there dumbly, her eyes wide in shock at developments.

I was sore around the throat where she'd clutched at me, but I was gloating all the same. My strategy had tripped the trigger that released a flood, not only of tears, but of revelation. There was undoubtedly more to the story, but it would come out now in its entirety. I'm always amazed how genealogical research of past events can solve crimes in the present. What a life I'd chosen for myself.

But what about Buck? Poor Western North Carolina Genealogy Society President Buchanan "Buck" Bradford. He didn't know what to do, who to turn to. His prime supporter and wife of many years was a killer. At least, that's how things looked.

Franks pulled a radio from his belt and made a call. "Delta-31. I've got a female suspect in custody for homicide. Requesting unit for transport."

But the drama wasn't quite over. Vivian suddenly sprang into action again, this time at a run toward the floor-to-ceiling fourth floor window. Those windows were in there solid though, and I knew that when she hit, she'd merely bounce off. But I was wrong.

The hotel was slated for some refurbishing. One of the identified problems was the mounting of those suicide preventing windows. Some of them were loose. This was one of them.

When she hit, the dense mass of her traveling at speed popped the glass pane out of its frame and sent it sailing off into the cool morning air like a magic carpet. She was right behind it, like a crash test dummy.

The pane hit the ground with a shattering crash, immediately followed by a dull thud.

Buck, Franks, and I went and looked out of the window frame. People were already starting to gather around the broken corpse of the late Vivian Bradford McIntyre Bradford, self-confessed murderess.

In minutes the corpse was surrounded by uniformed officers. A sheet was thrown over her so the guests wouldn't be upset.

During their marriage, Vivian had come to realize that her husband Buck, though a clever fellow and a respected working genealogist, would never amass the fortune that Vivian would have liked. He was a working class guy with the basic and respectable working class goals of earning a living, keeping a roof over their heads, and food on the table. In this, he succeeded. But Vivian had tired of her humdrum day-by-day life and wanted more.

When a book contract worth $100,000, along with all the accompanying perks and hoopla, suddenly appeared on the horizon, Vivian decided she wanted it for Buck. She knew that he would never try to get it, being content where he was in life with his freelance research work. She took matters into her own hands and devised a plan which, in the end, hadn't worked out as she'd hoped.

The New York publisher Filgurst had awarded the contract early on to Nadia. Vivian had never liked Nadia. Perhaps it was jealousy over Nadia's good looks, her outgoing personality, her constant bevy of interested men. Whatever it was, Vivian knew she had to get Nadia out of the picture. She told her nephew, Oliver Bradford Cobb, to scare Nadia off.

But Ollie was a bit too enthusiastic with his length of pipe, and Nadia's skull hadn't been as thick as mine, and she had been unexpectedly killed. Was it murder? Was it manslaughter? That would have been decided at the trial. But Ollie, the prime suspect, was never caught. He never got the chance to stand up in front of judge and jury to plead his case, to plead for mercy, to point an accusing finger at Vivian as the instigator of events.

Ollie's death had been inadvertent. Murder? Manslaughter? Death by misadventure? This time, Franks had his perp, but it was too late for the courts to decide her ultimate fate. Civilization had been saved once again. And court costs, too.

And in the end, it was all for nothing. Later that morning, Filgurst, a quiet middle class kind of guy, upset by the confusion and mayhem at the convention, lost his sophisticated veneer and scrapped the book project altogether. He'd had enough of these North Carolina weirdos and on the earliest Sunday flight he could get, returned to the New York City craziness that he understood.

Chapter 24 – Dénouement

Sometimes people kill for revenge. Sometimes for love. Sometimes even for pleasure. Sometimes it's momentary insanity brought on by circumstance. Or it could be self defense, defense of one's family, home or lifestyle. Sometimes people "just need killing," as folks say, or because the killer is just a mean S.O.B. Viewing humanity from the perspective of the outsider I've always been, it's almost understandable. Not likeable, and perhaps not pardonable, but almost understandable.

And when it comes to killing, we humans are wonderfully creative. It's one of our species' greatest talents, perhaps even the single characteristic that most clearly defines us. You might think of the basics like shooting or stabbing. Defenestration is good sometimes. That's simply throwing someone out of a window like Vivian did to herself.

How about exsanguination? That's another great label for a specialized killing style. I wonder who comes up with these terms of art. That means to bleed someone out. You can do it with a knife or a razor. And people do it to themselves all the time when their rope's run out. It's the classic bathtub wrist slashing.

Then there are various poisons: strychnine, cyanide, and arsenic are venerable oldies. Modern medicine provides lots of opportunities in this area. How about not poisoning as such, but using drugs to kill nonetheless by withholding meds that are keeping the prospective victim from sliding into the abyss? A new subtlety for the knowledgeable. A less informed rural murderer might stuff a rattlesnake into the prospective victim's mailbox for laughs.

If you're squeamish about doing the deed yourself, you can always hire a hit. There are lots of folks around with minimal scruples, or sociopaths to whom life doesn't matter. A few bucks invested in the project and your troubles are over. It's not like you did it yourself. Instant deniability. "How could

I have done it, detective? I was in a bowling tournament in Cincinnati at the time. Hundreds of witnesses. I was half way across the country on live television when it happened."

Let's be clear though. I'm talking about personal killing, not mass political killings like war or genocide. I'm not thinking about Pol Pot, Stalin or Hitler. The truly interesting deaths are committed person to person. That's where we find real human interest, the kind that sells newspapers and propels crazed nobodies to immediate media stardom.

The most popular reason for killing someone, the one I've seen time and again, is simple greed. One of the Big Seven: the Seven Deadly Sins. But in that list, greed is third. I'd put at the top. Wanting more, of whatever, even if the perp already has plenty, drives the world in its dizzying revolutions through the Cosmos. But honestly, how much is enough? What drives a person to acquire more and more, to pile it up or stash it in mattresses or tax-free municipal bonds, and perhaps to the detriment of his or her fellow humans? I don't get it. I guess that's why I'll never be a "success," never own a Rolls-Royce or a Rolex watch, never murder someone for the last chocolate chip cookie on the platter.

This time it was greed and pride that drove Vivian Bradford, the nothing much wife of a relatively unknown but respected genealogist, to murder. Her goal, to win her husband a publishing contract worth $100,000 and gain him a more prominent title than the temporary presidency of a minor genealogical society out on the fringe of civilization in Western North Carolina. She wasn't doing it for herself, not directly anyway.

Vivian Bradford had planned to fix things so her husband won the publisher's contract, but she wasn't much of a party girl and all the hoopla that went with the contract would be wasted on her. She would have been content to bask in the reflected glow of her husband's glory. It was a Lady Macbeth sort of plan, or like something conceived by the conniving women in the Kurosawa film *Ran.* The blood on Vivian Bradford's hands was for the benefit of another person, and would have only benefited her because of association. You might even call her plan altruistic in some twisted sense.

Her plan had been simple at the start. Her nephew Ollie was supposed to scare Nadia into leaving, but he'd hit her too hard and killed her by mistake. Ollie's death had been another error, a mistake caused because Vivian's frustration and anger had flared at the boy. She'd struck him only once, but it had been a killing blow.

And in the end, what did she win? A sudden trip through a defective window all the way to the ground without an elevator. She ended up with a good deal less than nothing for her scheming.

In any event, I was headed home in one piece, back to the usually predictable big city mayhem of Atlanta. This weekend I'd learned a bit about some tricky genealogical techniques as well as more about human nature, and I'd been involved in another hair-raising adventure. As I like to say, a genealogist's life is fraught with danger.

Asheville, North Carolina might be a nice place to visit, and even to live, but not this particular weekend. Still, I'd been thinking of leaving Atlanta. Maybe...

But for now, I was headed "home." Another job well done. Well, done, anyway. Whew!

Appendices

Containing information relevant to the story, genealogical charts, Theron R. Quince's lecture handout on bastardy bonds, and copies of digitally archived legal documents on record that are related to the Bradford/Lester bastardy bond proceedings.

Appendix #1 – Convention Program

3rd Annual
Western North Carolina
Genealogical Convention

at the
Asheville Pisgah Hotel
in
Asheville, North Carolina

May 24 – 27, 2012

Presented by
Western North Carolina
Genealogy Society

Attendees

Check the bulletin board at registration throughout the convention for the latest schedule changes and personal messages.

Exhibitors & Vendors can be found in the Davidson Room. Please patronize our vendors.

Please set all mobile electronic devices to silent or vibrate for all sessions. Respect your sister/brother genealogists.

Thursday Night Mixer

On Thursday evening the Lineage Links Genealogy Society and the Buncombe County Genealogical Society will host an open bar for presenters, panelists and vendors in the Vance B meeting room. This event is limited to pass holders. (Pick up your pass at the conference registration desk.)

Sessions & Presenters

Thursday

Time	Session Title	Presenter(s)	Location
6pm – 9pm	Registration & credentials	WNCGS Staff	Lobby
	Social Mixer	Cash bar	Vance A
	Presenters' Mixer	Complimentary Bar	Vance B

Friday

Time	Session Title	Presenter(s)	Location
8am -	Breakfast Buffet	-	Vance A & B
9am	Registration & credentials	WNCGS Staff	Lobby
9am	Keynote Address: Genealogy – America's Fastest Growing Hobby	Nadia Worthington-Lamond	Merrimon
10am	Dangers of the Hunt: Genealogical Adventures	Benjamin S. Bones	Merrimon
10am	Digital Photography for Researchers	Gavin Sprint, Ph.D.	Vance B
11am	Etiquette for Genealogists	Rosalba Post	Vance A
11am	Bastardy Bonds	Theron R. Quince	Vance B
Noon	Lunch – On your own		
1:30pm	Interviewing Family Members	Porter Thibideou	Vance A
1:30pm	File Organization	Pleasance Reethe	Vance B
3pm	Wills & Probate Records	Filo Remondier, Esq.	Vance A
3pm	Church Records	Rev. Odel Parnassus Salmon	Vance B
4:30pm	Launching as a Pro	Panel	Vance A
4:30pm	WNCGS Business Meeting	Buck Bradford Members Only	Room 101
6pm	Dinner – On your own		
7pm until	Mixer	Cash bar	Vance B

Saturday

Time	Session Title	Presenter(s)	Location
8am –	Breakfast Buffet	-	Vance A & B
9am	Registration & credentials	WNCGS Staff	Lobby
9am	Plenary Session	Buck Bradford	Merrimon
10am	1940 Census Data	NARA Rep.	Merrimon
11am	Finding Maiden Names	Paula Roland	Vance A
11am	Manumission vs. Emancipation	Xavier Gibson, Jr.	Vance B
Noon	Lunch - On your own		
1:30pm	Military Pensions	J. Willoughby, Col. Ret.	Vance A
1:30pm	Placing Ancestors With City Directories	Orville Twitchell GA Historical Soc.	Vance B
1:30pm	Internet Research	Fanny Quinlan-Bolton	Merrimon
3pm	Reconciling Death Certificates & Probate Records	Dr. Emanuel Whalen	Vance A
3pm	21st Century Genealogy	Barry Singer	Vance B
4:30pm	Proving Native American Ancestry	Rosa Blue Sky	Merrimon
4:30pm	Identifying and Dating Photos	Gavin Sprint, Ph.D.	Vance A
4:30pm	Unfindable Ancestors	Cedric Michaels	Vance B
6pm	Convention Banquet	Ticket holders Only	Vance A & B
7pm until	Mixer	Cash bar	Vance B

Sunday

Time	Session Title	Presenter(s)	Location
7am - 8am	Breakfast Buffet	-	Vance A & B
8am - ?	Closing General Session	Antigone Killian-Groome President Emeritus	Merrimon

Appendix #2 – Lecture Handout on Bastardy Bonds

Bastardy Bonds in North Carolina

The concept of the bastardy bond was brought to the American colonies from British law. It's very simple. The county in which a bastard child is born does not want to pay for the maintenance of the child. To avoid this, the mother and, where possible, the named father, are made financially responsible by law, specifically, by posting a bond.

The legal steps to establishing a bastardy bond run in a straight line process. Information is provided to the court that a woman is either pregnant with or delivered of a bastard child. The mother is summoned to court to be examined as to the circumstances and to identify the father. If the mother refuses to name the father, she can be fined and perhaps find herself jailed.

If the purported father is named, he is then summoned to court and he, or his sureties, are obligated to provide for the child by posting a bond of however many hundred dollars are the named price at that time in history. If he refuses, he can be fined and/or sent to jail until he accepts the reality of his situation and commits to support the child.

In all cases, the mother's name is known. That's why in traditional Jewish law, the family line descends through the mother, not the father. Simple practicality. The father is occasionally unnamed, as when the mother refuses to reveal him for some reason. Known names appear in recorded court documents. Unfortunately, the child's name is rarely, if ever, recorded but for genealogical purposes, knowledge of the parents' names is usually enough to determine lineage. The child's age might be mentioned as well. Sometimes the child's name appears in contemporaneous or subsequent apprenticeship documents.

Ben Bones & the Conventional Murders

Before Emancipation, it was common enough for a white male to impregnate a slave woman with no consequence in regard to acknowledgement of or support of the illegitimate child. Things changed after Emancipation. Depending on the location and/or the history of relations within a particular county, the situation might have changed a great deal or very little. The various North Carolina counties tried to hold men, white or colored, responsible for their progeny. But this was not an equality issue. It was strictly to protect the county financially.

Records of court bastardy proceedings can be found at the North Carolina State Archives (see References below).

Legal Process for Bastardy Bond

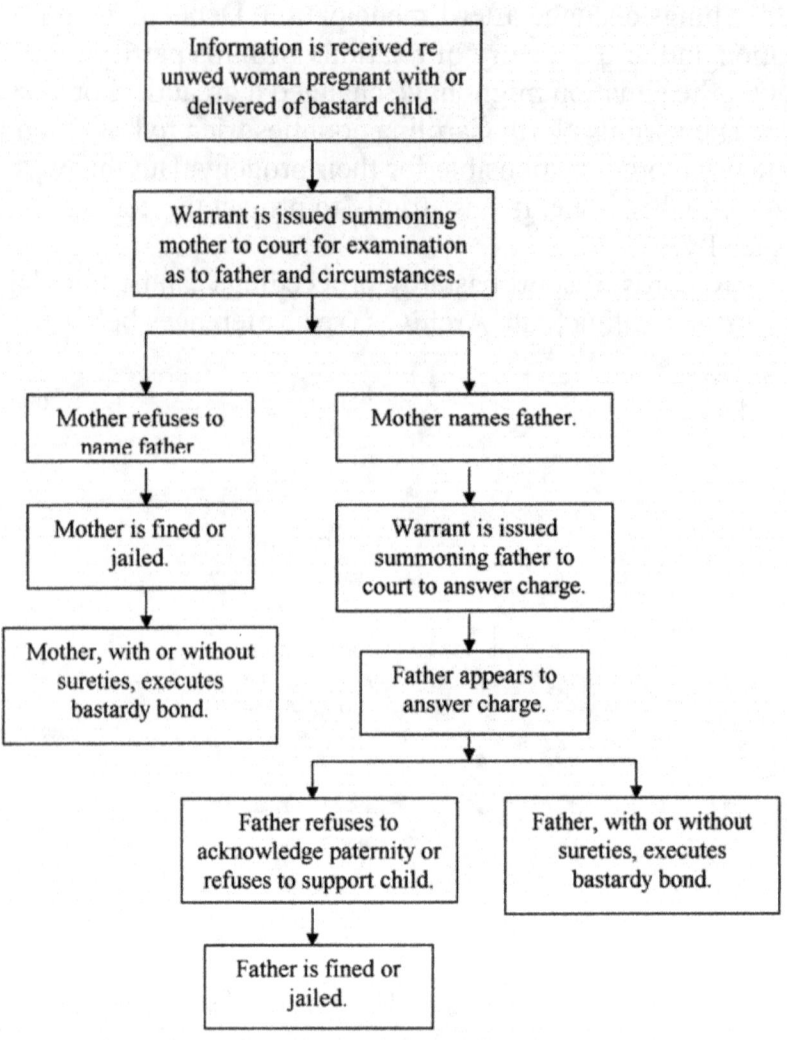

Information is received re unwed woman pregnant with or delivered of bastard child.

Warrant is issued summoning mother to court for examination as to father and circumstances.

Mother refuses to name father

Mother names father.

Mother is fined or jailed.

Warrant is issued summoning father to court to answer charge.

Mother, with or without sureties, executes bastardy bond.

Father appears to answer charge.

Father refuses to acknowledge paternity or refuses to support child.

Father, with or without sureties, executes bastardy bond.

Father is fined or jailed.

References

North Carolina Bastardy Bonds
Transcribed by: Betty & Edwin Camin
252 Pages, 8.5"x11", Full Name Index, Perfect Bound,
NC-0144, $35.
P.O. Box 400, Signal Mountain, TN 37377

Johnston County Bastardy Bonds
Copyright © 2009 Warren T. Bagley
http://www.rootsweb.ancestry.com/~ncjohnst/bastardy.ht
m

*Bastardy Records of Tyrrell County, North Carolina 1791
– 1879*
George Merritt
http://patriot.net/~cpbarnes/tyrbbond.htm

Bastardy Bonds
Posted by Dave Tabler | November 3, 2011
http://www.appalachianhistory.net/2011/11/bastardy-
bonds.html

Suspect Relations
by Kirsten Fischer, Cornell University Press, 2002
www.infouga.org/site/

North Carolina State Archives
http://www.archives.ncdcr.gov/county_definitions.htm#b
onds

Nash County, NCGenWeb
www.ncgenweb.us/nash/

*Illegitimate Children and Their Parents Mentioned in
Nash County Court Minutes 1787 to 1835*

From readings of the records by Dr. Stephen E. Bradley Jr. and Timothy W. Rackley in their series, "Nash County, North Carolina, Court Minutes Vol. 1 to Vol. 13. Please consult the original books and/or the original records for complete citations.

"Matters of bastardy normally include the mother's sworn statement of paternity (generally mentioned but not transcribed) and an order for reputed father to support the child to some extent. The child's name and gender are rarely given, although its age or time of birth may be. Bastards took the mother's surname–a child referred to as John Smith of Mary was almost certainly illegitimate." Fines were levied so public was not charged for private misconduct but court could alter, extend or rescind its orders. Bastard children were, in most instances, apprenticed to others to learn a trade. (from "North Carolina Research: Genealogy and Local History" by Helen F. M. Leary, Ed.). The apprenticed changed over the years as the child grew to legal age, thus the person you are interested in may be listed more than once.

Appendix #3 – Descendant Genealogy of Dixon Alton Bradford

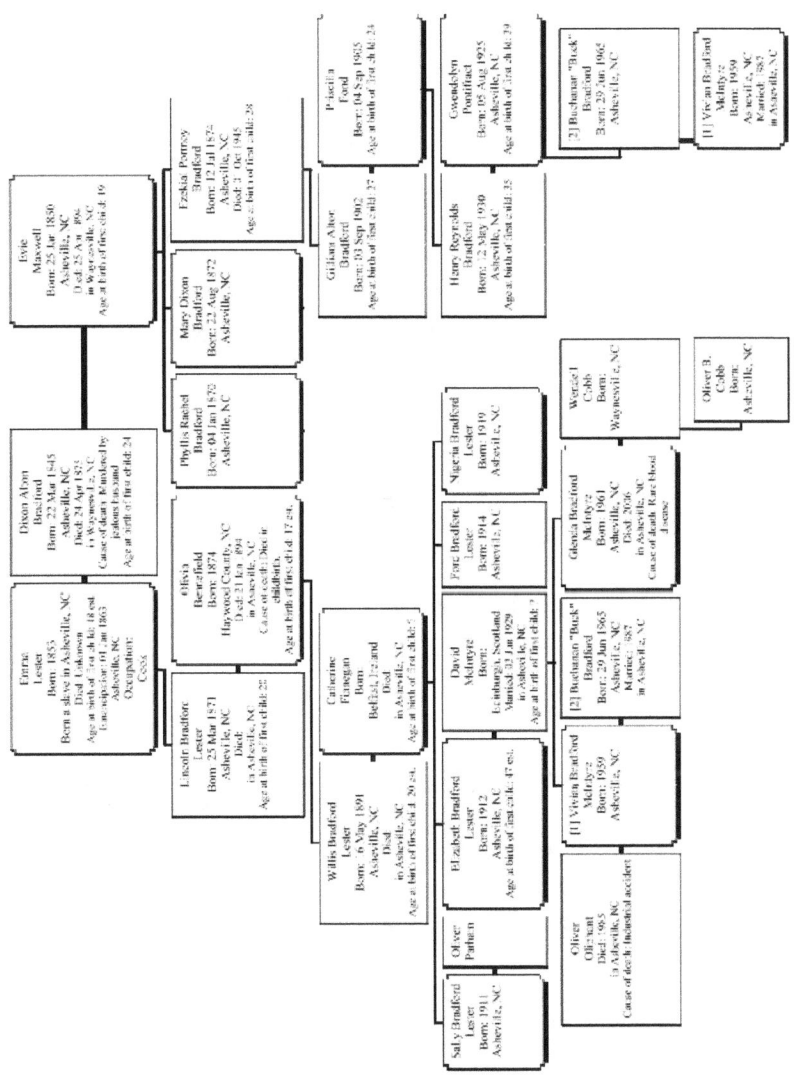

Appendix #4 – Descendant Genealogy of Emma Lester

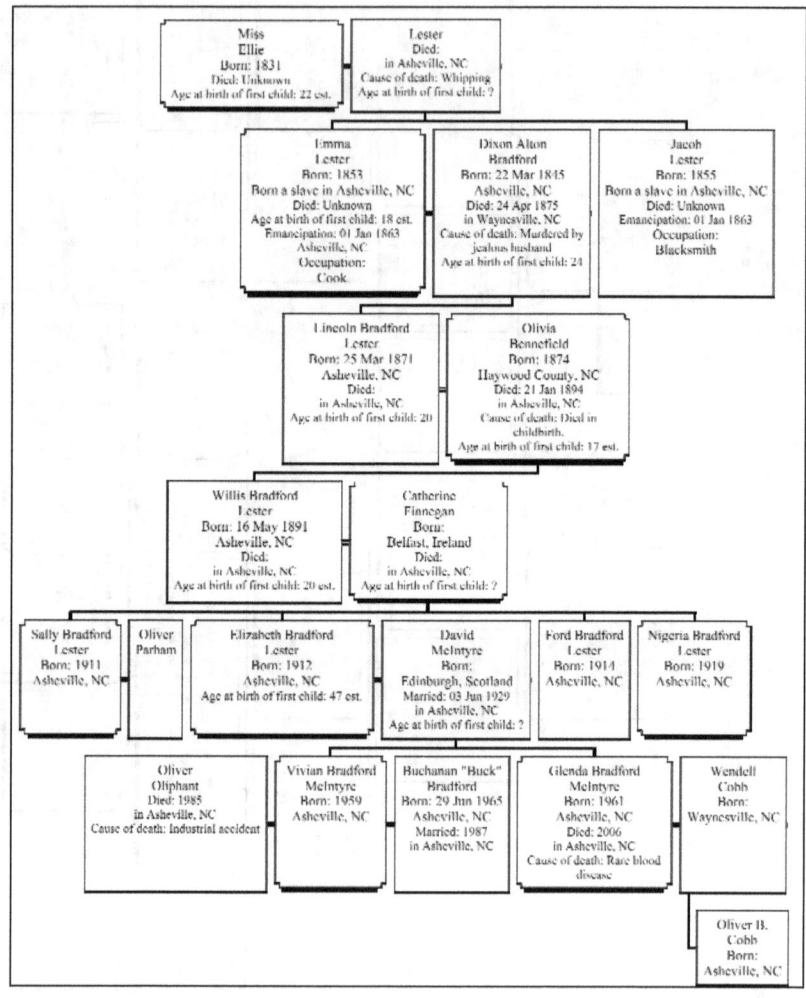

Ben Bones & the Conventional Murders

Appendix #5 – Pertinent Bastardy Documents

Information Against Emma Lester

State of North Carolina}
Buncombe County

To any lawful Officer

Whereas information hath been made to us two of the Acting Justices of the Peace for said County, that Emma Lester (col) a single woman hath been delivered of a Bastard Child, and which child may become a charge to the county.

These is therefore to command you to forthwith cause her to appear before us or some two Justices for said county, and there to answer the matter, charged against her as aforesaid.

Given under our hands the 20th day of April 1871.

D. E. Freeman JP

Andrew Farnsworth JP

Warrant for Emma Lester

..........*Buncombe*.......... **COUNTY** : -- *Justice's Court.*

STATE

Against *Emma Lester*   }   **Warrant.**

THE STATE OF NORTH CAROLINA, *Buncombe*.......... County

To any Constable, or other lawful officer of said County, Greeting:

Whereas, *information hath been made to me, one of the Justices of said*

county, that ... *Emma Lester* .... *of said county, is with child,*

which, when born, will be a bastard, and may be chargeable to the county. These

are therefore to command you to apprehend and bring before me or any Justice of

the Peace for said county, the said ... *Emma Lester* ....,

to answer the matter alleged against her as aforesaid. And this shall be your

warrant.

Witness my hand and seal. *April 24, 1871*

Andrew Adams .... *J. P.*

Emma Lester's Declaration of Reputed Father

The State of North Carolina,

..........Buncombe.......... County – Justice's Court.

Before.......... L. R. Sawyer .... J.P.

On this 26. day of .... April .... 1871., the undersigned, a Justice of the Peace in and for said county, proceeded to take examination of .... Emma Lester (col) ...., whereupon she declares upon her oath that ...., [illegible handwriting] to .... [illegible handwriting]

She further declares that .... Pinson Allen Bridges .... is the father of her child.

.... Emma Lester (col)

Taken and subscribed before me this 26. day of .... April .... 1871.

.... L. R. Sawyer .... J.P.

Warrant for Dixon Alton Bradford

WARRANT AGAINST THE FATHER. - Printed and for sale at Harrell's Cheap Job Office, Henderson, N.C.   No. 107

Buncombe **COUNTY** : -- *Justice's Court*

STATE

Against *Emma Lester*

}
}
}
}
}

Warrant.

THE STATE OF NORTH CAROLINA *Buncombe* County

To any Constable, or other lawful officer of said County, Greeting:

Whereas, upon the examination of *Emma Lester (col)* this day taken on oath before me, it appears that she *is delivered of* child, which child, a bastard, and may become chargeable to the said county, and the said *Emma Lester (col)* hath confessed that *Dixon Alton Bradford*, of the county aforesaid, did beget the said child, and hath charged him with the same: These are therefore to command you to apprehend the said *Dixon Alton Bradford*, and bring him before any Justice of the Peace for the said county, to answer said charge. Given under my hand and seal, this *26* day of *April*, A.D. 187*1*.

L. R. Lowrie J. P.

Capias Order for Dixon Alton Bradford

Bastardy Bond (with Sureties)

THE STATE OF NORTH CAROLINA,

.... *Buncombe* .... County.

Know all men by these Presents, that we *Dixon Alton Bradford,*
our .... are held and firmly bound unto the State of North Carolina
in the sum of .... *Five* .... hundred dollars, for which payment we bind
ourselves, our heirs, executors and administrators, jointly and severally. Signed
and sealed this ... *9* ... day of .... *May* ...., A. D. 187*1*...

Whereas, the said .... *Dixon Alton Bradford* ...., stands charged
with the maintenance of a bastard child, begotten by him upon the body of ....
.... *Emma Lester* (col) of said County;

Now the Condition of the above Obligation is such, That if the said ....
.... *Dixon Alton Bradford* .... shall perform the order of the
Superior Court of said County concerning the maintenance of said child, and
indemnify the said County from any and all charges for the maintenance of the
same, then the above obligation is to be void: otherwise to remain in full force and
virtue.

.... *L R Cooper* .... [SEAL]

.... *Jno C Montague* .... [SEAL]

.... *Willie B* .... [SEAL]

Test: .... *Joshua Clark*

Author's Backword

We often see a forward written by an author to explain himself. This usually comes before the substantive text of any work. In this case, I wanted to tell the story of *Ben Bones and the Conventional Murders* first, then to do a bit of explaining.

People have asked me where Ben Bones came from. It's time to clear the record, to reveal the truth of his birth and evolution, to "out" him fully.

Some years ago I was living in Atlanta, Georgia. One day, a sister Mensan said she was headed to the National Archives to do some genealogical digging. I'd done no genealogy on my family to that point, but being a Mensan and abnormally curious about anything and everything, I went along with her. The trip was a revelation for me. I was introduced to the 1920 U.S. Census and even discovered my missing biological grandmother, a woman I had never thought about before.

It must have been a few days later when I realized that I'd been acting as a detective by delving into my family's history. From there I realized that any genealogist would be working as a detective. But suppose, just suppose, that a genealogist was called in to solve a problem for people in the present... a problem that had its roots in the past? That was an "aha moment!" for me, and Ben Bones, Consulting Genealogist and Articulator of Family Skeletons, was born. And I knew I had a serial character, too.

I've read several mystery series. Many have a story line that repeats or the action happens in the same place all the time. I determined to vary my stories and, to attract a wider audience, I planned to have Ben go to different locales for his adventures.

The first story, *Ben Bones and The Deadly Descendants*, happens in Rome, Georgia. I was working there at the time and could walk around town to find interesting locations and historical facts. I used Opera Alley, the local library and its genealogy section, the office of *The Summerville News,* and the

Chattooga County Courthouse, amongst other hot spots. I visited a hospital trauma room and a nearby state jail facility and got tours at both places. I even discovered a town that no longer existed. How could I not use that?

Ben's second adventure, *Ben Bones and The Search for Paneta's Crown,* is sited in Savannah, Georgia. I used my legal training in that story. The plot centers around a vague reference in a will and a missing family artifact that Ben is called in to find. The inheriting siblings all want the artifact for themselves. Ben finds himself in the middle of their plotting and scheming, a dangerous place to be.

When I moved to Asheville, I decided Ben needed a North Carolina story. A bit of research showed me the dangers of the ocean off Cape Fear. Perfect! I drove east and built the story around a 400-year old Spanish treasure ship that was wrecked there. It's fiction of course, but the facts fit the true nature of the area. I had lots of fun with that book.

And now you're holding *Ben Bones and The Conventional Murders*. Someone said I needed an Asheville adventure, so I sent Ben to a genealogical convention here for some "professional development." It turns out that there's skullduggery afoot in a tangled family history involving bastardy bonds in North Carolina, and in professional rivalry over a $100,000 book contract, too.

Yes, Ben Bones is a geek's geek. But so am I. Ben gives me the opportunity to learn about arcane topics. He teaches me about genealogical research as I follow his tracks through history and back to the present. Facts are facts, and my research is solid. Stick with us and you'll learn a good bit, too.

Other Mysterical Adventures

by
Michael Havelin

Ben Bones & The Deadly Descendants

Ben Bones & The Search for Paneta's Crown

Ben Bones & The Galleon of Gold

The Extra Body

Palaver's Hands

Bloody-Minded Fictions

And for folks who want to learn to write mysteries:

*Mystery Mastery:
Creating a Believable Mystery Novel*